Piranhas & Quicksand & Love

Piranhas & Quicksand & Love

Stories

Sally Shivnan

Press 53
Winston-Salem

Press 53, LLC
PO Box 30314
Winston-Salem, NC 27130

First Edition

Copyright © 2016 by Sally Shivnan

All rights reserved, including the right of reproduction in whole or in part in any form except in the case of brief Quotations embodied in critical articles or reviews. For permission, contact publisher at Editor@Press53.com, or at the address above.

Cover design by Maryam Banyahmad
and Amir Khatirnia
www.behance.net/amirkhatirnia

Author photo by James Gerfin

This is a work of fiction. Names, characters, places, and incidents are products of the author's imagination or are used fictionally. Any resemblance to actual events, locales, or persons, living or dead, is entirely coincidental.

Printed on acid-free paper
ISBN: 978-1-941209-42-4

For Jim

and remembering Alan Cheuse, teacher and generous soul

Grateful acknowledgment is made to the editors of the publications where the following stories, some in a slightly different form, first appeared: "Dicking the Buddha," *The Antioch Review*; "The Confectioner," *Glimmer Train Stories*; "Simon's Berth," *The Chesapeake Reader*; "Something, Anything," *Rosebud*; "Dee Told Bea," *Perpetuum Mobile*; "The Mover," *The Baltimore Review*; and "Lola," *So To Speak*.

The book referenced in "Rapture" is *Sailing: a Lubber's Dictionary* by Henry Beard and Roy McKie, published by Workman Publishing, 2001.

Contents

Dicking the Buddha	1
The Confectioner	19
Simon's Berth	29
Piranhas & Quicksand & Love	41
Something, Anything	59
The Detectorist	65
Blood Lake	77
Dee Told Bea	91
The Mover	101
What Do You Remember?	115
The Accidental Inventor	125
Rapture	145
Lola	167
Bit and Piece	179

Dicking the Buddha

I waited for my sister to sit down, before I asked her. Then I waited a respectable moment, while we sipped our coffee and looked out the kitchen window at the vinyl siding of the house next door. There is nothing interesting to look at out the windows of my sister's home. I set my elbow in something sticky on the tabletop; I didn't look down but shifted myself discreetly.

"Would it be okay," I asked, "if I borrowed the baby?"

"Again? Jesus Christ, Tabby"—she looked toward the living room to see if her two-year-old had heard her swear—"this is getting to be a habit."

"Only for about three days."

"Four days. It's four days."

"Well, back that morning, on the fourth day. Or I could bring him back the night before but it would be really late."

My sister Lizelle is strong, angular, with a nice clarity about her. She looks like the pictures of our mother, who was a perfect likeness of Lauren Bacall only black. Actually, biracial, mulatta: our mother's mother was black, her father white. Lizelle could pass for our mother in those photos, including the look of her skin—color of a heavy rainy sky.

I don't look like anybody, except I have the same narrow, elegant nose our father has. He, too, is half-black and even lighter-skinned. My skin is like his; people think I look ever-so-slightly different, exotic, often ask me where I'm from. He lives on the other side of the country now, with another woman, and our mother died a long time ago.

There at the kitchen table, in her capris and bedroom slippers, Lizelle's legs, I noted, were ashy. Her lips were dry and bitten. She had once plucked her eyebrows but hadn't in at least a year and they had grown in thick, glowering, a perpetually pissed-off look. I knew she'd say yes. I knew she'd let me have the baby.

"Mikie has something to do with all this, doesn't he?" she said.

"Only as inspiration."

Mikie is our brother, a former entrepreneur who lives in a large RV and follows the lawnmower racing circuit, towing a trailer for his souped-up Snapper—the only thing stranger than my mama as Lauren Bacall is my brother the redneck good ol' boy. He says he's like that pioneering black cowboy, Bill Pickett, except he's on a lawnmower instead of a horse. He reinvented himself this way when he sold his internet startup company for a heinous sum shortly before it went bust. He sends cryptic postcards from obscure towns across the south, always addressed to both of us, 'dear Tabby and Lizelle,' or 'dear Lizelle and Tabby' though they only come to Lizelle's address.

"That whole 'dicking the Buddha' thing, I still don't get that," Lizelle said. "It still bothers me." Around the time Mikie went mobile, he started teasing us about it: What do you do if you meet the Buddha on the road? I don't know, Lizelle said, feed him? ask him stuff? I had heard something about killing him, but from the wicked twinkle in Mikie's eye I knew this wasn't where we were going. A ninth-century Zen master, Mikie explained, name of Lin Chi, advised killing the Buddha if you ran into him, to keep yourself from getting too caught up in celebrity worship. But if you *really* met the dude, Mikie said, bumped into him, just like that—I tell you what now, don't dick the Buddha! When we asked him what that meant he just laughed, looking like a redneck Buddha himself with his beer belly hanging over his Snapper belt buckle, and his bizarre attempt at a mullet haircut. This was what money had done to Mikie. He's an asshole and I'd just as soon he stopped sending the postcards.

"I don't get it either," I told Lizelle. "But I don't really care anymore."

"That's what worries me."

Around us on the floor were toys, clothes, sippy-cups, an old baby blanket somebody had been dragging around. I wanted to point these out to her and say, *this* is what worries *me*, not this exactly but what goes along with this, what goes into the bargain.

"How's Ty?" I asked. Ty is Lizellle's husband. He is deployed with the army in Afghanistan.

She shrugged. "Okay. Everything's okay. I get emails."

"How are you getting along with Monica?" Monica is Lizelle's mother-in-law.

She frowned into her coffee, her eyebrows lowering like a storm, their pissed-off look mutating to enraged. Just then the two-year-old started dropping things on the baby, who was asleep in the playpen—small, soft things but enough to wake him up, but in any case it was time to pack everybody up and go get the four-year-old from preschool, and so we spoke no more about it, except to agree that I could come pick up baby Cody the following day.

Just a few hours south and what did I see but a Bradford pear in full, blinding white bloom—small tree, size of a Mini Cooper, a perfect oblong in shape like a giant genetically engineered baking potato. It was my first sign of spring, which I was driving straight into. Then the tree was gone and I was back to staring at I-95, heading into Richmond, the baby conked out in his car seat behind me.

Cody's seat faced backwards, so to see him I looked in two mirrors: a baby-view mirror attached to my visor, aimed at a second mirror hanging on the back seat, facing him. His pacifier had fallen to his lap, he had a little drool from the corner of his mouth, and his tiny right hand rested upon his armrest in a delicate, aristocratic way.

The truck drivers smiled down at me, smiles that were friendly rather than leering only because they saw the baby in the back. I had the whole thing going, bundles of Pampers, cases of Enfamil, bottles and plush toys and rattles lying all around the car, the little sunshade suction-cupped to the window, the 'Baby On Board' sign. It was a small but distinct pleasure to fool people this way.

I had watched my sister, handing over Cody. Watched her turn into the all-aflutter mother: *You have the right diapers? You have enough formula? You remember what I told you about the A & D ointment, how I stopped using that other stuff?* We'd stood in the driveway, beside the open door of the car. It was early, the sky starting to lighten, the air cold, soft dew on the grass. The first cars were creeping down their driveways to begin their commutes. All the houses were boxy, stark, the trees small. I watched the upstairs windows of the house across the street light up, one and then another and another, while I stood there with Lizelle, waiting for her to let the baby go. Cody was in a traveling outfit—she had dressed him up—sweatpants and a shirt with a bear on it, and a little blue wool hat, and little sneakers that seemed so unnecessary and sort of heartbreaking. She lifted his foot and studied his shoe, pressing the shoelace into some more perfect shape, and I tried to hold still and not look like anything that could be interpreted as impatience, or anxiety, or regret, or anything else.

Lizelle was supposed to put Cody in the carseat but her eyes welled up and she held him close and just stood there. She pressed her nose to the top of his head and inhaled his smell through his hat. Then she looked up and her tears were gone.

"I can't do it," she said.

Shit, I thought.

"I can't," she said. "You have to do it." She passed him to me and we made eye contact just for an instant—her eyes were hard, clear—and then I turned to settle Cody in his seat. My last view of my big sister, as I pulled away in the car, was of her walking slowly back up the driveway to the house, her long arms wrapped around herself like a straightjacket. She paused to look back at us, then drifted up the driveway a little, paused again, then drifted again.

In all his affluence, what has Mikie done for Lizelle? I watched her walking away and I knew I didn't owe him a thing.

Fourteen hours later, I was settled in a motel room in Georgia, surfing the cable TV, the baby asleep at my side. The sheets had a clean but harsh feel, and the tropic print bedspread had a faint solvent odor about it. But it felt good to be inside a room, stretched out, the TV on, the air conditioner throbbing along. I had set the three locks on the door—deadbolt, chain, and doorknob—and pulled the drapes. There is nothing in the world quite like the anonymity and seclusion of a cheap motel room, which is identical to the anonymity and seclusion of thousands of other motel rooms all over the country, each with a different person hidden in it, each with his or her own story. I let the TV rest on the Weather Channel and lay there looking up at the swirl-patterned ceiling, tracing the edges of old water stains through the swirls, and thought about all those people in motel rooms everywhere but couldn't quite wrap my mind around them. I felt sure that they, too, would not be able to imagine me.

It had been a long day, all the way to Georgia, with all the stops I had to make to feed and change the baby and play with him, roll him around on a blanket on the grass or bounce him on my knee at a rest area picnic table. I wanted him to have a quality life while he was with me—it wasn't his fault he'd been brought along.

The long day of driving on that single road burned images into my mind, of springtime: redbuds flowering all down the edge of a stretch of woods somewhere in the Carolinas, a single pink magnolia at some rest area, just four feet tall, blooming hard as if to make up for its size. Medians with daylilies planted in them (not blooming yet but big lush clumps of foliage, lined up in neat rows like lettuces—back home their leaves were just poking above the ground). But there was also the noise of hundreds of billboards and exit signs, crowding my mind with their crass insistence about what I needed at any given time. And people at the gas stations and rest stops, all passing through to somewhere, fat guys in big sedans, prissy white girls in their daddies' SUVs, Wal-Mart mothers with screaming kids, hollow-eyed stoners in beat-up cars.

The people behind the counters at the gas stations were often black folk with deep, deep southern voices—it reminded me how our people are from Carolina, the black people, that is, on both sides. Lizelle and Mikie and I are not a very family kind of family and we're not in touch. Our parents weren't into the down home thing. They read Alex Solzhenitsyn not Alex Haley. They lived in Paris for a while when they were younger though they came back to Philadelphia to have babies. Our dad dated a series of white women after our mom died.

It was Mikie who learned, when we were teenagers, that children born to two mulatto parents are still technically mulatto. They do not qualify as quadroon or octoroon or any of those fractionated categories. Of course, these are very old-fashioned terms.

I lay in my motel bed remembering how a pair of grandmotherly black ladies had walked by a bench at a rest area where I was feeding Cody, and how they stopped to coo and smile at him, and how I joined in the smiling, and looked up and saw a kind of love in their eyes for me.

I banked the extra pillows around the baby to keep him next to me, killed the TV and the lights and curled up with him. I thought about my sister and my brother. How everything to Mikie was just a big joke, nothing to take seriously. I wanted to say to him, Lizelle's husband in Afghanistan is not a joke, and her alone with three small children is not a joke. Her stuck there with three little kids and her old man not only gone but an asshole as well—not a joke.

I could hear Cody's breathing. I kept my eyes closed, waiting for sleep. I remembered Lizelle: bright, shining eyes, red lipstick mouth, sitting cross-legged on her college dorm twin-size bed, in her tomboy flannel shirt and her big gold hoop earrings and jangly bracelets, with Peace Corps brochures, of all things, spread before her. I said, Lizelle, look at you, are you serious? What I meant was the lipstick, the bracelets, the fondness for dancing and vodka gimlets. I couldn't see her in the Peace Corps and I told her so. And this is the great thing about my sister—she laughed. Laughed and rolled back on her back, saying Tabby, Tabby, it's the *Peace* Corps, it's my *calling*, both of us laughing then because it sounded so funny and high-blown. I didn't feel bad for what I'd said because I knew it wouldn't stop her dreaming, that she'd move on to something else, something equally big and wonderful, with or without me. Like all siblings, we had our family roles to play—I was the bratty kid sister, the spoiler, while she was the schemer, the visionary. She did the dreaming for both of us.

I thought about my phone call to her—her idea, not mine—from a gas station in South Carolina. I leave my cellphone at home on these trips, because of the whole GPS tracking thing, which I'm a little paranoid about. The call was short, she was stoic: "How is everything?" she said. "Just fine." "How's Cody?" "He's an angel." "All right then…" I stood there holding the greasy phone away from my chin, staring at discarded soda cups and plastic wrappers in the grass, imagining her beautiful redbone-Bacall face turned to stone by her reality.

The Florida panhandle is a musty old place that cries out for a feather duster—nothing Orlando or Miami about it. Spanish moss on the power lines, standing water in the ditches, long chip-and-tar roads through endless pines with mirages that dance in the distance, always flickering out and reappearing farther on. Air so thick you want to stand still to breathe. Towns so small the speed limit never changes, stays sixty right on through, maybe a Baptist church and a couple of shacks and you're gone, over some blackwater creek with no name, across railroad tracks that disappear in their straight line into nowhere, something beautiful about the rust-colored rails against the dark green of the pines.

This was where I was, after a second long day of driving. Then came the part I hate, turning off the pavement onto the long packed sand roads that run like a maze through that forest. Something about losing the asphalt under me makes me feel ill and lost. I had the air conditioning on, all the windows up, because it was warm and airless even as the sun was going down but also because I didn't want to be there. When I stopped and got out I didn't turn off the car, I wanted the engine sound so I wouldn't just have the screaming reeling of the insects in the trees, and I wanted that reassuring vibration against my body while I leaned there, waiting. My heart was pounding and I couldn't really see anything though my senses felt as if they were on fire. I told myself, this is a safe place. I stood with my back against the car, one ankle crossed over the other, casual.

When the other car came it was the same guy as before, to my relief, a clean cut young Latino who looked like a medical student. We worked quickly and without speaking, swinging the gym bags from his trunk to mine. It was all over in minutes and I was driving again, the first miles on dirt like something out of a horror movie because I'm thinking, if somebody knew, if somebody wanted to get what I had, they would do it here, on one of these forestry roads that thread their way into woods and swamps nobody has ever seen. On the pavement I started to breathe a little but all I wanted dear God was to get to Tallahassee and feel the interstate under me again.

I am ashamed to say I did not think about Cody through all this. I had given him a little Benadryl at the last place we stopped, something I would never tell my sister, but then, there was a lot here I would never tell my sister.

So then I'm on I-10, heading back toward Jacksonville. It was dark and there was a kind of comfort in that, the cloak of night around me, the people in the trucks and cars not real now, just lights in my mirrors, points of red receding, or white approaching. The road was quiet, lightly traveled. I had the cruise control pegged to the speed limit, so people passed me, singly, at long intervals. It was a calming road. I was exhausted, all the adrenaline drained out of me. And I had been in my car all day for two days and my body felt broken—feet so tired of being down there on the floor, back sore, shoulders tight. All I had to do was get to the other side of Jacksonville, to some motel room with a big bed.

I thought about the guy back in the woods. Thought about my Toyota backed up to his old Chevy sedan, both cars still running, the taste of exhaust in my mouth. The weight of the bags—how they swung through the air, the feeling of the fabric handles digging into my fingers. And as I pushed at them in my trunk, to make room to pack others against them, their chilling solidity, their density. The dude's face was completely neutral, serious—that's why he looked like a medical student, it was like he was performing some procedure: slipping a scalpel into a patient. He wore khakis and loafers—his shoes were shiny, which looked strange there on the dirt road—and I only looked down and saw his shoes like that for a moment, but noticed how his feet shuffled like ballroom dancing as he swung the bags across, so that he wasn't a doctor to me then but a dance instructor, which fit with the clean pants and the shoes.

Maybe it was his cover just as Cody was mine. I guessed my encounter with him didn't qualify as meeting the Buddha on the road. Don't dick the Buddha!—every postcard from Mikie is signed with this. We just read them and throw them away. He could quit sending them anytime and it would not break my heart. He could send money instead, now there's an idea, money for Lizelle, money for *me*. "What does it mean?" Lizelle used to ask me. "What happens if you dick the Buddha?" "Bad karma, I guess," I'd say. "Though I'm not clear," I told her once, "if dicking him means really fucking him over or simply failing him in some lesser way." "The Buddha could take any shape or form," she said. "He could look just like you or me. How would you know him?"

Lizelle gets a wistful look in her eye sometimes when she talks about Mikie, and I know it's because she envies his freedom. I envy him his money and his luck, and I told him this once, and he said money and luck were the same thing. Like me, Mikie has tried many things, with gaps in between. He knows a lot of people. He's the one who set me up with all this, made the phone calls, asked me no questions about it. I wish he *would* ask—why are you doing this? what is it for? If I knew where he was, I could send him a postcard: *ask me about it* is all it would say. It's for

Lizelle, you asshole, is what I want to say. I would not add what I know to be true in my most honest moments, that it's for me too, fuck yes, of course it is. Who am I kidding when I pretend it isn't? Only myself, but there must be a reason I pretend.

Across the median, on the other side of I-10, on the shoulder, I saw lights ahead, police lights, pulsing red and blue behind a splash of white light which at first was just that, a spot of light in the dark. I came up past it and I saw, the way you do, figures frozen in the light which then were gone: a black man standing before a white cop, another cop pulling everything out of the trunk, making a pile of it on the ground. I clicked down once on my cruise control. I watched the scene recede in my mirror, the three men swallowed again into light, the hard white light and the pulsing red and blue growing smaller and smaller. The lights turned to points, and wobbled in my rearview mirror the way stars do when you try to fix them through binoculars. My hands were moist on the wheel.

Our motel room that night reeked of cat piss, and there were male voices arguing through the wall, but I was not about to complain. I went back and forth, bringing in the bags from the trunk, with Cody on one arm—I couldn't put him down on the piss-smelling floor or on the bed where he might fall off, and I was nervous about leaving him in the car out there, even for a minute at a time. Bringing in the bags made me nervous too but it was safer than leaving them in the trunk. I lined them up down the edge of the bed, a barricade for Cody while he slept.

By the time I was done he was waking up from the Benadryl, late for a feeding. I fixed him a bottle and started to sit down with him, but I was so tired of sitting I got up and sort of slow-danced him around the room, pissy rug and all. The guys next door lowered their voices, and a train went by, not close but not far off, and I swayed, gently, the way it feels natural to do with babies, and listened to it. I closed my eyes, and the train faded, and all I heard then was Cody sucking his bottle, and I felt like his mother—it happens sometimes. Holding him there like that, feeling his weight in my arms, eyes closed and hearing only his contented suckling but picturing him, his perfect face, his hair, his skin, I felt he was mine.

Cruising up I-95, my long, long home stretch, milky Florida dawn giving way to wide open Georgia morning, bright blue cloudless sky, easy traffic, mostly tractor trailers, all passing me and smiling, taken in as usual by the sweet young mother pulling off the big road trip with her baby, and all I could do was smile back, yes, gentlemen, you got it, that's me, supermom. I had some R&B station on the radio, a styrofoam cup of coffee to sip on, and Cody in the back doing what four-month-old people do best, sleep. That is, until he started waking up, except it was too soon for him to wake up, I had just fed him and changed him, and he didn't wake up gurgling either the way he always did but gearing up to cry. I thought, okay, okay, we'll check you out at the next exit, but then his crying started and it didn't sound like his crying, it was this high-pitched, thin, scary thing, and I looked at him in the mirror and his face was really red. I turned around to see him, talk to him, felt around behind me for a pacifier, found one on the seat, stretched to try to get it in his mouth, trying to keep my eyes on the road, had to turn around to try to reach him with the pacifier, couldn't reach. Lizelle, I thought, Lizelle, calling her name in my mind because she would know what to do. Up ahead I saw no exit, no signs for one, nothing, just straight road running past a lot of big pines. God, I thought, shut up! The noise was outrageous, it was killing my ears. I thought, fucking babies! What am I doing with a fucking baby! It was so selfish to *scream* like that, in my *ears*. He was an ugly screaming alien monster—I thought, what have you done with Cody? He needs his mother, I told myself, but she was hundreds of miles away, and suddenly I knew I had done a terrible thing taking this child and that's when I saw the flashing lights in my rearview mirror.

I pulled over, felt a sickly crunch of gravel under my wheels. The cop did not get out of his car right away, was calling somebody or running my tags or something. I gave Cody the pacifier, and he settled down to whimpering.

I was terrified—this was, of course, the possibility I had always dreaded, for which I'd rehearsed in a half-assed way, but now that it was here it seemed unreal, unbelievable, yet somehow inevitable at the same time, though I had no thoughts for it, no words, I was just *there*, sitting, staring through the windshield at the place where the grassy verge down from the shoulder ran into the pines, the thick brown bed of needles beneath them looking unaccountably soft.

The officer leaned down by my window to talk to me, to look inside my car. He was a state trooper, a big white guy, a television cop with the crisp uniform and southern drawl. He had shiny black boots. He had a substantial beer gut. He had a large gun.

He had stopped looking at my license and registration but did not hand them back to me. "You were driving erratically back there, miss," he said. "Do you know why that was?" I couldn't tell if I was supposed to answer, or if he was about to tell me. So I didn't say anything.

"You want to tell me why?" he said.

"The baby," I said. "My baby. He was crying and he wouldn't settle down—he didn't sound right—I was worried—I'm sorry, I got distracted by my baby." Cody, now, was fast asleep.

He looked down at me and I looked up at him and my eyes filled with tears. "You need to be real careful when you're driving, young lady, keep your attention on the road, for the safety of yourself *and* your baby."

"Yes, sir, I'm sorry, I'm so sorry." He looked like he could be a father himself and I had the strangest urge to grab onto him then and have him take care of me and little Cody. Even though I was still scared shitless and even though he was a big white ugly Southern policeman.

"Don't be sorry, be safe." His voice was stern, and I felt very small. But he handed me back my license and registration, and I knew all at once he was going to let me go. He asked me where I was headed. I told him I was going back home to Pennsylvania. He said it would be a good idea if I didn't try to drive back there in one day, seeing how I was alone with the baby and all. I agreed but didn't commit myself. I was trying to not say much of anything.

I watched him, in my side mirror, walking back to his car. He loped, as if the gun weighed him down. Thank God, I realized, that he didn't have a dog—one of those ones they steer in a circle around your car like a poodle at a dog show. I had never thought of this before. I was shocked that I hadn't.

My capacity for stress was spent and I drove like a zombie and in a very straight line, the radio off, wincing at every twitch the baby made. The desire to stop was overwhelming—to pull off at some exit, into some gas station parking lot, turn off the car and just sit. But it felt safer moving than sitting still and I was too scared to stop until I had to. The picture of the cop, in my mind, stayed with me, and his voice, too. I thought, are you the Buddha? but I doubted it.

After a while I got to feeling that I'd come through the fire, that the test was behind me, that money and luck were on my side and nothing else bad could happen, but I was wrong, and when I did stop, to feed Cody and buy gas and eat a peanut butter sandwich, I collided with a situation I was completely unprepared for, unprepared in part simply because I was so played out, so drained from the day's events, plus it all happened so fast—but I know I am rationalizing.

The gas station was busy, people waiting their turn at the pumps. After I bought my gas I moved the car over to a parking space by the convenience store, and relocated to the passenger seat, where I sat with my feet out the door, Cody in my lap slurping at his bottle and staring at me in a meaningful way. It was warm, with a little breeze over us. The big windows of the store were bright and full of signs offering deals on Mountain Dew and breakfast burritos and Sunbeam bread. The glass doors opened and closed, people rolling out clutching the things they'd bought. I was sitting there thinking how safe I felt because there were people around me.

I started remembering, for some reason, Lizelle's husband—I think it was the crying Cody had done earlier that made me think of this, because my memories of that man are caught up with the sounds of children crying and fighting—I was seeing him in profile, in front of the television in his old brown recliner, drinking cheap canned beer, the two-year-old and the four-year-old doing some bratty fussing at each other on the floor, ignoring him. He ignored them too, was focused on the TV, but was not relaxed—his recliner was kicked halfway back but he strained forward, his muscles tensing through his tee shirt, the sleeves of which were cut off as if to give his big deltoids more room. He looked like he was about to attack the TV, pound it to pieces. And then he was yelling *I smell shit in here! This kid needs his diaper changed!* never taking his eyes from the television screen. I wondered, as I often do, what he would be like when he returned from Afghanistan.

And that's when I looked up, distracted by some noise, to see a white girl with a baby beside a rusted station wagon, across the empty parking space between us—close enough we could have taken one step toward each other and touched. She was standing there, by the driver's side door, which was hanging open. She couldn't have been more than twenty, was skinny, bony, and pale as death, and the baby was smaller than Cody, just a month or two old, wearing a diaper and a grubby shirt. She held the baby against her chest, while a man—as thin as she was but older, with long stringy hair—staggered at her and hissed at her. Each time he lunged near she twisted away, as if to protect the baby from blows—his hands were in fists at his sides.

She wore a faded red tank top and cut-off shorts and flip-flops, and had long blond hair. Her eyes flashed a mixture of defiance and fear, but these emotions on her face were older than she was, older than her eighteen or twenty years—her anger and fear looked old and hard. I couldn't take my eyes from her face.

He kept hissing at her—did not raise his voice—I couldn't make out what he was saying. But she got louder, and her voice was shrill, girlish—*Cut it out! Lay off of me! Leave me the fuck alone!*

He grabbed her arms above the elbows—his wiry hands clawing into her—and she stumbled and nearly dropped the baby, and the sound she made then, catching up the tiny baby, was something I cannot describe—a desperate, short, forlorn, animal sound, the most plaintive thing I have ever heard. He pushed her into the car, stuffing her through the door, and got in after her, shoving her across the seat, and he started the car, staring straight ahead. He backed up, and the car swung so that for two or three seconds they were facing me—she was silent, her mouth set in a hard line, her eyes beady and terrified and staring straight into mine.

They pulled away, tires squealing. The people around me seemed self-conscious and subdued (this, however, may have been my imagination), but no one was looking in the direction of the car.

It had happened fast, but I could have done something—but I didn't. Of course, I would not have endangered Cody—but I could have started yelling, making other people notice, while I moved away, out of the way, with my baby. The sight of me, with Cody, yelling, would have forced them into doing something, making a scene that would have given that girl a chance, a choice. I did nothing, because at every single instant, the hard bright fact burned in my mind that I needed to get north, in the straightest line available to me, no turns, no risks. No more lapses in attention, threats to concentration. Even as that car pulled out of there, I knew I would not act—would not try to imprint on my mind the make of the car, the numbers on the license plate—instead I made my eyes a blank. I would not call the police from a payphone. I knew this even then. Even as that girl's gaze locked with mine through the windshield of the car, and then broke, as the car turned and she kept staring ahead.

Beside me, as I drive, the trees fall away, the land opens up, and endless flat pasture runs off to a line of dark pines in the distance. I see a clay track, leading a long way through the grass to a trailer set at a random angle, the only human mark out there.

I shuffle my thoughts, like cards, like prayers. Get this poison out of my car. Stop the postcards. Kill that bastard in Afghanistan. Do not maim him.

An exit sign explains the overpass ahead, just one town's name on the sign, and no gas, no food. The off-ramp rises beside me, passes by, I fly beneath the bridge and it is gone, and I do not even wonder where the road goes—all those empty two-lane roads that cross mine at right angles and disappear.

I come past farm fields freshly disked for spring, the earth folded open in raw, brown rows beneath the sun. Dusty, poor-looking land, sharecropper dirt that some distant dead sister of mine may have pushed a mule through. I cannot feel her, though. She is someone else's story. It makes me think of my parents, who gave me what I am and what I am not. Where we come from, far, is not where we come from, near, and I think about that boundary between near and far in my family's past, and I wonder where it is and I have no idea. I think of what crossing that boundary has made us: crazy Mikie gone over to the rednecks, Lizelle in her military-wife suburban hell, and me, doing this.

And I think of Lizelle and I think, *it's for you, it's for you, it's for you.*

The Confectioner

The old man was bent over with his hands deep in the display case, touching the tops of all the chocolates, noting their smooth, rounded corners, their uniform peaks, his fingers brushing the tickly edges of the paper cups as he moved from the maple creams to the vanilla butter creams, and then to the orange, lemon, and coconut ones. His hands trembled up to the cordial cherries, over the flat pieces of almond bark, alighting on the meltaways. It was a great relief, the bending down, like a rubber band relaxing, though reaching with his arms was a strain. He peered into the sunlit depths of the big glass case. His was a view like looking through crystals of rock candy.

The bells on the door jingled: it was a customer (the teenage boy who worked for him came in, always, through the back door). The old man jerked back from the chocolates and pulled himself upright. He laid his hands on top of the case, avoiding the hazardous shapes there, the gift bags hanging on their little tree, the jar of giant lollipops, and the pyramid of fancy little tin boxes which customers could buy and fill with chocolates.

A woman walked up to the counter, smiling. He knew

her, she was after peanut butter smoothies. She had been coming in for several weeks. She always moved quickly, always in a hurry.

"How are you?" she said.

"Very well," he said, mumbly.

"I'll just have two peanut butter smoothies."

He obliged her, and took her money. He put the bill in the cash drawer and held out a dime to her. She waited a few moments. The light changed around her as the sun came out from behind a cloud. A truck went by and the window shook.

"I gave you a five dollar bill," she said, gently.

He nodded and murmured and opened the drawer again, and took out four single bills and gave these to her without apology. The bills fluttered as they left his hand.

"Thank you," she said, looking at him, staring.

"Very well," he replied, inaudible then as another truck went by.

But after the truck passed, the room was silent. The old man took up his position behind the glass case and stood motionless there. He heard the jingle of the bells again as the door was pulled open. He stooped again as the bells ceased, reaching deep into the case once more to touch where he left off. His fingers found the almond butter crunch, then he patted the chocolate mini-pretzels, lingering on them. But the woman had paused in the doorway, thought to return, closed the door, and was studying him, wide-eyed, as he pawed the chocolates with his trembling hands.

He heard the bells again. He straightened immediately and faced the door. He waited but nothing happened.

"Hello?" he said.

He stood there until his back ached from the strain. The clouds crossed the sun again, changing the light.

"Hello?" he tried again, but then he heard his employee coming in the back door, and forgot his confusion. He remembered, instead, how he needed to talk with the boy, because he was so deeply worried about what was ahead of them, though he doubted the boy had given it much thought.

"Danny," said the man.

"Mr. Feathers," the boy responded.

Danny nodded at his boss and set himself to wiping up the frosting on the table; he'd left it there when he got hungry, knowing he could clean it up when he got back. Stretching over the table made him burp onion from his sandwich. He had offered, as he always did, to bring the old man something back for lunch. He had never seen Mr. Feathers eat anything but a piece of candy, once or twice a day.

Just now Danny looked over and saw him insert a cream into his mouth. The old man turned, facing him, chewing. He saw the boy had stopped work, was standing upright and still; he cleared his throat and said, "Would you like one?"

"No," laughed the boy, and went back to wiping the table. "I tried to bring you lunch," he said. "You never eat nothing."

Danny's arms made wide, smooth arcs over the table's surface. He wore a football shirt, smudged with chocolate, which hung to his bony knees like a dress, hiding the cut-off shorts he wore underneath. His skinny ankles stuck out of basketball shoes that wore a perpetual fine white crust—the sugar grit and flour dust were everywhere, creeping out of corners and coming up from the cracks of the linoleum tile. The steel legs of the table where the boy was working were thinly dusted, even the walls of the place, and the old man's desk and chair, and the old man! Danny wasn't blind to it, but left it be.

Mr. Feathers remembered that he was worried and he shuffled over to his little desk and stood with his nose almost touching the calendar on the wall. He was able to make out the month because he already knew what month it was.

But he was thirsty after eating the chocolate. His tongue stuck when he tried to lick his lips. He began to move to the sink to get a glass of water, a substantial journey because his steps were small.

Danny bumped into him on his way to the sink to rinse his rag, said "sorry" but too softly for his employer to hear. They stood side by side while Danny washed the icing from the rag and stared out the window, whose glass, like everything else, wore a dusting of white, only thick enough to make the world outside a shade paler. He didn't look at the daffodils blooming in the dirt-patch beneath the window, but straight to what interested him more, the back lot of the used car dealership down the block, where the cars were washed and waxed before they were moved out front. He admired the gleam of red and chrome and glass, shiny even from this distance. Mr. Feathers began waving his arm in the air over the sink.

"What is it? What do you want?" Danny asked, but didn't get an answer. Eventually the old man managed to say "water," though Danny, by then, was across the floor with a broom, sweeping, and did not hear him. Mr. Feathers continued to reach for a glass whose location he did not know. He touched the faucet but didn't turn it on. He tried to say, "I want a glass of water," but it came out of his throat as just a croak. His arms grew heavy, so that they started sinking in the air as he reached with them. A burning came to his eyes, but he was too dry to make tears. Danny had danced off with his broom to the front of the store—the old man noticed how distant the sweeping sound was.

He gave it up and returned to his desk to sit down. Danny came back and stood looking out the window again, leaning on his broom. At lunchtime, he had walked across the gravel lot he stared at now, had felt light, hungry, had felt the warm sun on his shoulders, the nice openness of space around him. He sighed, turned away from the window. He made a decision.

"I'm going to make the fruit paste," he said. He came over to the sink, took down the big stainless steel bowl. Mr. Feathers sat quietly in his chair while the boy moved around the room, making noise everywhere, like the sounds of a woman in the kitchen—the ring of a bowl coming to rest on the table, the fall of a spoon in the sink. The old man remembered the photograph on his desk and began to gaze at it in a dreamy way—just like the calendar nearby, he knew the photograph because he already knew it, a picture of his wife and daughter, Judith and Isabel, who had both died a long time ago. Across the room, Danny studied the old man studying the picture. The daughter had died first, then her mother. Danny had no idea when this was, and it hadn't seemed right to ask. In fact, Mr. Feathers wouldn't have been able to answer. With the passage of years, the two losses inched ever closer together in time in his memory, and if pressed he would not have been able to describe his wife and daughter, their hair, their eye color, their ages when they died, the sounds of their voices. "Judith and Isabel," he thought.

The boy rolled out the candy dough on the table. He stretched forward, his shoulders unbinding, loosening, his forearms tensing, his hands tight on the rolling pin. His flat belly pressed the table's edge. Come summer there wouldn't be much to do there. People didn't eat chocolate in the summertime, it melted when the weather got hot, they bought ice cream instead. His friends expected he would quit that job when things got slow.

The old man stirred. He remembered what he was worried about—Valentine's Day was behind them, Easter was coming. He began to speak and Danny had to pause in order to hear him.

"It's time to change the sign," he said.

"We don't have to do that yet," Danny said.

"No, it's time to change the sign."

"I'm in the middle of this, it'll have to wait."

Mr. Feathers thought about the situation. He knew it would take the boy a long time to finish. The sun was moving around to the back window, and the rear of the store, where they were, was warm yellow with the light. Time was slipping away, and he was alarmed—the boy, though, never seemed concerned about important things.

"I'm going to go change the sign," Mr. Feathers said.

Danny frowned, said nothing. He had a lot to get done that afternoon and only so much time to do it.

The letters for the sign were kept in a plastic bucket underneath the desk. Mr. Feathers picked up the bucket and started for the front door, while Danny continued rolling out the candy. Some moments later the bells hanging on the door jangled stiffly as Mr. Feathers passed out of the building.

He walked the few steps to the sign, and set the bucket down. In his ears the continuous noise of the street carried on—the rising and falling sounds of cars approaching and then fading away, the vans and trucks rushing by. At times, the sounds were complex—brakes and horns, and trucks working to shift up or down—there were two lanes in each direction, and traffic lights both ways. The trucks lifted dust from the road and left the smell of diesel exhaust behind. The old man tasted the street in his mouth.

He began pulling the letters off the sign. His arms were slow but he didn't have to reach high. The bendy plastic rectangles, each printed with a single black letter, came easily out of their grooves; he dropped them in the bucket. The sign rested on wheels, and had an electric arrow that pointed toward the building and which would light up if it was plugged in, but they never plugged it in. It was of the same sort as two other signs farther down the block—the one at the church, whose message changed each week—GOD GIVES ENOUGH GRACE FOR WHATEVER WE FACE—and the one at the car lot, which never changed—USED CAR BLOWOUT. A few feet above the electric sign hung another, older sign, wooden with tin letters, sticking out over the door of the store. It said *Candy Shopp*, its vestigial *e* long gone.

Once Mr. Feathers had cleared all the words from the sign he stood still a moment, looking at its white emptiness. The bucket beside him was almost full to the top now with letters. He bent down and pulled up a handful, and he held them up one by one to his eyes. He found an L and an O and dropped the rest back in the bucket, and fitted the two he kept to the top line of the sign. He reached down again, slow, and brought up more letters, his face flushing red now and his breathing huffy as he worked to make out the shape of each one. He found another O and an exclamation point he kept as well. His body swayed as a tractor trailer went by, and he dropped the exclamation point on the ground. He would leave it there for now. He stooped again to the bucket: the bend in his knees made his whole frame shake. He managed to lift just one letter. He straightened. The letter was not anything he could use.

The next time he pushed his hands down hard on the letters in the bucket and clamped his fingers around them. He forced his legs straight. He breathed through his mouth, in and out, too fast. Half of his letters fell to the ground. He held onto the remaining ones and stood there, waiting to feel better.

Danny left the table and went to wash his hands at the sink. He shook his head, frowning, picked up the towel to dry his hands, looked out the window, stared at the gravel. He began to move away but then stopped, stayed a moment longer, gazing out the window at nothing. He patted his hands with the towel, then balled it up in his fist and threw it down sharply on the counter.

He went out front and saw Mr. Feathers standing there, face to face with the sign, blinking, panting. His fists hung at his sides like weights, each grasping a letter. The sign said LOOK OUT and that was all.

Danny stepped forward. He scratched his head and then stood with his hands on his hips.

"What are you trying to spell?" he asked. He saw all the letters lying around the man's feet. He picked up the bucket. When the old man didn't answer, he said, "What letters do you want?"

Mr. Feathers gasped, "B."

Danny flipped through the bucket, found a B, began to insert it next to LOOK OUT, but Mr. Feathers said, "New line."

He started a second line.

"What is it you're trying to spell?" Danny asked again. He could have worked more quickly if he knew, but the old man wasn't saying. Instead he puffed out the name of each letter with a difficult breath. Together, in this way, they built the words.

"Here," said Danny, "give me those," reaching for the letters the man still held in his fists. He had to lean down and unwrap his fingers from the letters to take them from him. Then he gathered up the ones lying on the ground.

"Come on," he said, and touched the man's elbow.

"No."

"Aren't we finished?"

"Yes."

"Come on then."

"No."

"What do you want?" He stepped back, put down the bucket, stood very still and straight while Mr. Feathers stayed bent over, wobbling. He looked like he might fall over, but the boy did not move to help him. "I have work to do," Danny said, "let's go inside."

"I have work to do," the old man echoed.

"No you don't. You don't have to do nothing. You just have to come in out of the street."

"No." His hands fluttered up to his head as if he was looking for his ears.

Danny grunted and looked around quickly. "I'm going then," he said.

"No!"

The boy stood and stared, with his mouth a little open. "Come on," he begged. "We look silly," he added, softly.

"I'm not silly."

Danny lunged forward, and Mr. Feathers saw the shape coming at him, the tall, strange body coming at him, and it made him fall sideways, his legs were gone, he had no legs, and he thought the boy was going to push him down.

But Danny caught him up in both arms before he quite hit the ground, lifted him, held him, their two bodies pressed close together, both out of breath. They hung together there, while the trucks and cars rushed by them trying to beat the traffic lights. They were close enough the man could see the boy's thin, smooth face, his eyes and nose, and the boy could see the watery redness inside the old man's lower eyelids, and the way they hung away a little from his eyeballs.

"I'm sorry," Danny whispered, drowned out just then by a passing bus, so that his whisper couldn't be heard.

He kept his arm around Mr. Feathers, steadied his elbows, and began to ease him toward the door. Danny looked back over his shoulder at their handiwork, as they took their tiny steps together. LOOK OUT, it said, BUNNIES ARE COMING!

The bells shook. The boy kicked the door shut with his foot. He continued to guide the old man, through the room, around the counter, to the little desk in the back, left him there and stood in the middle of the sunlit floor, his hands hanging empty, his head turned toward the window. Mr. Feathers could see his form in the haze of light—saw the boy was doing that standing-still thing he did sometimes. He waited for what the boy would do or say next.

Danny examined, briefly, the condition of his fingernails, then looked up at Mr. Feathers. He told him he had a mind to make some of those perfect little Belgian seashells, the ones with the swirls of creamy white in them all curling through the milk chocolate.

Simon's Berth

I was stretched out on the deck of the boat in a bikini, drinking a beer—it was not my boat, not my beer, and not my bikini. The afternoon was hot, sliding toward evening in that achingly slow, daylight-savings-time way. I was mostly in shade—the sailboat had an ugly, boxy cabin house that threw its shadow over the foredeck—and I was mostly out of view, because although it was a busy marina, I was docked at the swampy end, on a pier pretty far up the creek, the trees on the other side close enough I could have thrown a beer bottle and hit them. And the bow of the boat, where I reclined, was pointed out to the creek so a person would really have to work to notice me, which is what Simon did, standing there calling out, "Hello! Hello there!" as if he knew me, which he didn't.

I sat up and craned around to look.

"You look comfortable there!" he said. He was medium height, scrawny, lost in his clothes which were smeared with epoxy and paint and dirt, a real boatyard dog. Wiry-haired, unshaven, with a stupid grin on his face, a first-day-of-kindergarten grin. Maybe thirty, maybe thirty-five or even forty years old, I couldn't tell. Not a threat, I decided, just on intuition. Ordinarily, I would have slid back down out of view and waited for him to go away. But in those days, for a time, I thought myself reckless and free.

I offered him a beer. Why not? I thought—reckless, free. "Oh yes indeed, I thank you," he said. I reached into the cooler, and noted three bottles left. There was one more six-pack down below in the fridge. When that was gone in a day or two, maybe I'd be gone too, though I didn't know where. I was between jobs, between husbands, staying on a friend's sailboat, a dingy old fiberglass thirty-footer, nothing you'd look at twice, helping myself to what was lying around out of a sense of entitlement I had never felt before and have not since.

I stepped around the cabin house, stretched to pass him the beer, then retreated back to my spot, and stood there. I may have decided I wasn't afraid of him, but I kept my distance.

"Most grateful, most grateful," he said, twisting off the top. "On one condition, that ye permit me to return the favor." Was he hitting on me? He had the strangest voice—brassy but touched with the lilting shadow of some far-off, marshy Chesapeake island, Elizabethan and forgotten-sounding. Who were his people, I wondered on hearing it, and where had he come from?

I watched him take rapid sips of his beer.

"Permission to come aboard, Captain," he said.

"I'm not the captain," I said.

He laughed and stepped aboard but stayed where he landed—on the deck, peering at me over the cabin house. He continued taking quick little sips of his beer; me, I knew how to make it last.

He spoke of boats, warning me to watch out for that bane of boatyards, free advice, and he then proceeded to share a great deal of free advice with me, gleaned from his years of experience with his own boat, while I listened.

"Seven years I've owned her," he announced, grandly. It took me a second to understand he meant his boat. He'd paid too much for her, he said, though the sum he mentioned didn't sound like that much to me. He talked of leaks and fiberglass work and cabinetry, seemed terribly involved in her rehabilitation. "What a worthy boat she is, such beautiful lines and sturdy," he said. "I've little time for other things. I have to see the project through." He chided himself for taking so long, for not keeping more to the schedule he'd set. I responded that such an undertaking was bound to experience slow periods, that I was sure he had accomplished a lot already.

He wiggled his beer bottle in the air, eyeing what was left in the bottom, which was nothing, and smiling his goofy grin. "How be you fixed for these?" he asked. I gave him another beer and he kept talking.

A day or two later I saw the boat. It lay in the water, held in place by about twice as many docklines as most boats have, all of them necessary because every single one was frayed and rotted. It had no mast, or, rather, it had one, but it was lying lengthwise down the deck, overhanging the boat's bow and stern, presenting a hazard to passing boaters at one end and passing pedestrians at the other. In place of a mast, I suppose, it had a TV antenna, all criss-crossed bars and branches, jutting out from the deck at an odd angle. The cockpit was filled with junk, except for a narrow path kept clear to allow passage below—there were dust-laden bags of clothing and trash, compound buckets, tools, a couple of rusting propane tanks, anchors and chain and coils of rope, and miscellaneous pizza boxes and junk food wrappers, these last mostly stuffed between and into other things to keep them from blowing away. Along the deck my eye traced the courses of several large cracks that had been filled with caulk. Green tears streaked down from the ancient, corroding bronze ports. A splintered caprail followed the lines of the boat around, down its gracefully sweeping sides to its stern, where the old boat's form dovetailed to a modest and charming end; the slender railing was ruined, the grain raised badly, black grime embedded in every crevice. She must have been beautiful once. What had my new friend been doing these seven years?

Simon's boat was out on a pier at the other end of the marina from me, where the creek was wide and boat wakes and weather were an obvious problem. The slips to either side of him were empty—this was not choice real estate. I started strolling out there, every day or two, early in the morning when the place was quiet. The view out that way was clear, so if Simon was around I could take a different direction before I had to run into him.

One morning, just a few days after I met him, I noticed his mast was gone. Everything else on his boat looked the same. I started to head back and saw Simon walking out of the bathroom building, cinching the belt to his pants—long belt tongue flapping, old baggy pants gathered improbably at his bony hips.

I went up and spoke to him. He greeted me with his kindergarten smile. "What happened to your mast, Simon? I noticed it's gone."

He said the owners of the marina had made him move it up to the yard. He shrugged and explained he wasn't ready to step the mast again yet anyway. He went on to describe at some length the problems he was having with the marina management. He felt they were trying to pressure him, subtly, to leave the neighborhood. It was then that I learned that Simon's boat had been, in all the time he'd owned it, there at that one location, that he had purchased it there, and the most he had moved it was around the dock to a different slip. It had never sailed, nor been out of the water, in all that time.

"How long was it in the water before you bought it?" I asked.

"I have no idea," he said. I imagined its slimy, barnacle-encrusted, soggy underbelly, rotten as an old sponge.

The truth was the marina owners were not pressuring him subtly about anything, but were harassing him mercilessly on an almost daily basis. I figured this out a little from him ("Oh, ye know, they do like to keep at me, they have their wee issues"—he pronounced this 'iss-yooze'), and a little from a couple of the less-threatening types who worked in the boatyard (most were gorillas, not anyone I wanted to talk to), and also a little from a woman boat-owner who was around a lot and moved about the place like someone who knew what was what.

She laughed when I mentioned him. "*Oh*, yeah," she said. She told me how they had targeted his car as a substitute for his boat. They claimed it was dropping rusty parts on the parking lot and made him move it to the farthest, most inconvenient reaches of the property. They had him out there scrubbing the oil off the lot, which he had supposedly leaked there. They made him empty out all the boxes of junk from the backseat, claiming that the mess was an eyesore, and he ended up throwing most of it away, although he didn't want to. They had a shouting match about the muffler noise one day, which Simon, of course, lost. He walked to work for two weeks because he couldn't afford a new muffler, and then he lost his job and had nowhere to drive to anymore. When his tire went flat, Simon went out and changed it, even though he was no longer driving the car, just to keep the marina off his back.

"How do you know all this?" I asked her. She was a dirty blond, middle-aged, weather-beaten but attractive sailing type, with deep laugh-lines and twinkly eyes.

"He used to try to pal around with me a lot. I think he was sweet on me, but look at the guy—one look . . . Even he has to realize . . ."

One evening I was down below on the boat, trying to read—some paperback mystery I'd found there, but I couldn't get interested, nothing held my attention, the only reason I tried was that it seemed preferable to always staring into space—when I heard a knocking on the side of the cabin house, followed by the sensation of someone stepping on the deck—that heavy, sudden dipping. I guessed it was Simon, and I imagined him, reaching to knock but off-balance, having to step forward, onto the boat, to catch himself. I went out to the cockpit, and there he was. He looked like he'd been drinking.

"Have ye any of those beers left?" he said. If it were anybody else it would have been rude, but Simon was too pathetic to rate that.

"No," I said. It wasn't quite true, I had one left, which I was saving for something, I didn't know what, but figured I'd know it when it came along.

"I have a new job," he said. I already knew this, he'd already told me. It was at a garage a few blocks away. He took a few steps into the cockpit, plopped down on one of the uncomfortable molded benches, so I sat down across from him. He smelled of gasoline, and seemed greasier than usual.

"They're saying the boat's taking too long to near completion," he said. I knew who "they" were. "They say their insurance company has 'concerns' about my wiring. But that's ridiculous, I told them"—here he gestured expansively at the night sky—"because none of my wiring works. You think ye'd . . ." He shook his head, and lost his thought.

"What's going to happen, Simon?" It was what I'd wanted to know for some time now.

"They say they've had complaints."

"About what?"

"The work, at night."

He was referring to the noise of the grinder, that mysterious, brutal sound that erupted from within his cabin for hours every evening, except on weekends when it was already not allowed. On my late-night walks I had come close enough to hear it. I'd stand halfway down his pier, looking up at the stars and listening, completely unable to imagine what was going on in there. He never talked about it, I never asked.

"The grinder?" I asked, tentatively.

"They've told me all work on the boat, as long as she remains in the water, will have to stop."

"Maybe it wouldn't hurt to take a break—"

"They say they feel, for the good of the boat, that she could do with a drying out period up on land."

So, that was it. They were kicking him out of the water. His face twisted up, trying to think it through. He couldn't talk. I sat there and watched his face contort in the dim light. As long as his boat was in the water, it was a boat. In theory, though not in reality, as a boat in the water it could slip its docklines and sail to Fiji. Simon must have had dreams, beyond grinding his hull and sliming caulk into the cracks in his deck. I wondered what they were. I was looking at what seven years of dreaming had done to him.

He composed his face, and managed a smile. It wasn't the little-kid grin, but a pirate-smile.

"Mayhaps a season on land would be a good thing," he said. "I could get a look at her bottom and do any work it might need."

They had to tow the boat around to haul it out, since the engine didn't run. Simon acted goofy, clowning and giggling as he cast off the lines and floated out. They set the boat in an old wooden cradle in a distant corner of the yard, the very back row, just some scrap and brush and chain-link fence behind it, farther from his marooned car than ever. When they were all done, and things fell quiet, I walked over to see how he was.

The hull looked as bad as I knew it would, though I tried not to study it too closely. I went up the ladder—it was a decent ladder, the boatyard must have given it to him—and peered over the rail. Simon was sitting in his cockpit, wedged into a heap of piled-up junk. I surprised him, caught him with a blank look on his face—completely unregistering, completely unmoored—it embarrassed me to see it. He broke into his idiot-innocent grin when he saw me. I think it was only then that I saw that grin for what it was.

"Come aboard!" he said, brightly—as if I hadn't just caught the look on his face we both knew I'd caught. We did what people do: pretend. "Come aboard!" he insisted, though there was hardly a place for me to stand, and nowhere to sit down. I had never set foot on his boat and had no desire to.

"I'm okay right here," I said. I tried to look comfortable, standing on the ladder, leaning on his rail. "Here, this is for you," I said.

"What's this?" he said. "A beer!"

"A housewarming gift. You've moved to a new neighborhood."

"Ye are most kind. Ye'll have to let me return the favor one of these fine days." What's so fine about them? I thought, looking at the unbelievable piles of crap all around. What fine days are you thinking of, Simon? "Aren't ye having one yourself?" he asked.

"Nah. That's okay." I watched him twist off the cap and take three fast sips.

"Come on and see the boat," he said.

"I'm good right here."

"You've never seen her."

"I really can't stay. I have to go do some stuff." I wasn't flattered, exactly, though I was touched. "Why are you so anxious to show me?" I said, trying to laugh it off. I wondered if he meant the cabin below to redeem him in some way. Maybe his interior would be different from his cockpit and decks and hull. And I was curious about the nightly grinder noise. I was, in fact, more curious about him than I cared to admit. "Okay," I said. "Real quick."

I climbed into the cockpit and stood there, careful not to touch anything. Simon slipped down into the cabin and I took a step closer and peered in: every surface was covered with a fine white dust; tools and scraps of wood lay about, covered in the same dust, in places half an inch thick; spots that recently had been disturbed, either by the relocation of some object or by fingerprints or footprints, had just a thin layer, like new snow, upon them. So this was what the endless grinding had produced, though toward what end I did not know. Cabinets, half-constructed, lay off to one side. The engine, under the steps with its cover removed, was coated in the powder. The shapes of coffee cans and cups and bottles looked like sculpture set about in the snow.

Simon pointed at the plywood he had erected to block off the forward cabin. "I keeps the dust out of me bed," he said. "Works like a gem." He could see I looked puzzled. "I come and go through the forward hatch," he explained. Okay, I thought, so you don't *live* in the main cabin, you just grind away at the hull and make dust down there—you live in the little forward cabin, the V-berth. I was fascinated now—his space was getting smaller and smaller. He came back out and we walked along the deck to look.

I thought, how small can a home be and still be a home, still meet our definition of whatever that is? And not be, instead, a pretense, a delusion, a denial of homelessness?

I lifted the hatch and peeked inside. The smell rolled up: like turning over a deep pile of old dirty laundry. Below me lay a tiny nest padded with a grimy sleeping bag, a twisted, mashed-down blanket, and a single gray pillow. I saw hair, I saw grease smudges. Dirty tee shirts and pants and underwear were stuffed up against the sides of the cabin, and paper bags and empty soda cans. There was a small, very old television. An extension cord with a droplight—all the power on the boat, as far as I could tell—was led in through the hatch and dangled there above the bed. The smell was bad—I could almost see it, the fog of human breath and sweat and dirt.

"Okay," I said, standing up straight, pressing my hands to my back as if to say it hurt to bend down like that—it didn't, I was just trying to build a case for getting out of there. "Okay," I said again, feeling stupid. I couldn't look at him. I thought I might be ill. I stared out into the air across the boatyard. He stood there, waiting.

I tried to think of something to say, but politeness failed me, just didn't work, didn't apply, there was no way in hell. I was overwhelmed by a feeling, a vision, of the world pressing around that tiny and obscure space which day after day for seven years he'd folded himself into. Something made me turn to look at him then. His smile was hopeful and innocent but his eyes were knowing and sad.

I saw him in a new way, I saw him hiding like a mole in a hole, down in his filthy little bed, safe from the eyes of others—that was what this place did, keep him from view, closing off his body above, below, and around, so no one would be forced to look at him. And so he would not have to suffer their looking; so he could scream invisibly, silently, alone. Why had he shown me this?

I went to see him, on occasion, after he moved onto land—up on the "hard ground" or "the hard," as sailors call it. Each time, his little area in the back of the boatyard had a more lived-in look—more trash and cast-off objects that seemed to have gathered to him randomly: an aluminum lawn chair with the webbing half gone, a heap of coaxial cable, a stack of rusting paint cans. I had moved on and wasn't in the neighborhood much, so I was struck by the changes, and by the change in the weather, the seasons. Simon, of course, had not changed. As often as not, though, the few times I was there, he was off somewhere, working I suppose.

The leaves fell from the trees, and all the boats were hauled out of the water, rows and rows of them up on land, looking hulking and impotent stranded on their cradles. The docks were empty, the whole place turned bare and gray, just gravel and dust underfoot, a cold crunch as I would walk around. One day it was raining—that place did not look good in the rain. Other days it was just blowing cold, and there would be Simon's shipwreck, in its far corner in the back row. He had draped big sheets of plastic over it for winter, which made a great noise in the wind—I heard it before I saw it. The place was deathly quiet except for that sound. I'd stand and stare at the plastic, which he had tried to anchor with rocks and buckets full of dirt. It was to keep the rain out, but as much as that it must have kept the boat-sweat in. The great folds billowed and flapped like flags. Like sails flying loose from their cleats.

My life had changed, and I had less and less time, and less inclination, to return there. I looked back on my days adrift and was amazed that no real ill had befallen me. Each morning I sat at a table with a blue and yellow tablecloth, in a high-ceilinged kitchen full of cool winter sunlight, and ate cereal and drank tea, and thought about how it felt to be alive. It was odd to have survived something that at the time I hadn't realized I was surviving. It was a little terrifying, too, to think how I had fallen back into life as accidentally as I had fallen out of it. Sometimes I would think of Simon—as I dropped my cup in the sink, or gathered my things to head for the door—and I'd have an image of him sleeping in the bow of his boat. I'd think of him curled up in the dark alone, breathing the shallow, rapid breaths of dreams, and I'd wonder, how does he sleep, what does he dream? When he turns off the television, and the cathode glow fades into black, who does he think he is?

One day I went back there and he was gone. It was false spring—a breath of warm air that would go again, but enough to make you look into the trees to make out the buds. He wasn't in his spot at the back, or anywhere else. His campsite was gone. He had left no trace, no cast-off pieces of the boat, no junk, no trash, no shred of plastic. I could have asked someone, but I wasn't sure I wanted to find him or even to know.

I stood there staring at the lumpy, gravelly space where his boat used to be, and I tried to remember his face, the way you might with a lover you know you will not see again. And I couldn't remember it, of course, not exactly.

Piranhas & Quicksand & Love

Maria lives in a garden apartment complex called Lakewood, where there is neither a lake nor a wood and no one expects either. Its entrance sign is so weathered that the grain of the wood has raised right through the last of the paint and the letters are just ghosts, though Maria drives past without seeing it, because she is looking in her rearview mirror at her little boy's face. He is staring out the window but in a fixed way, so that everything passes his gaze without catching.

Earth to Justin! she wants to say but doesn't, because of all the terrible things other people say in front of him.

He squirms, makes a sound like clearing his throat.

"What is it, sweetie?" she says. The doctor has told her she should talk to him a lot. "Look at the tree," she says, but the spindly little tree is already gone. Lakewood is not much landscaped. "Look at the tricycle, layin' on its side." It is a badly busted tricycle, but she doesn't want to say that. "Look at the dog." The dog is lifting its leg on the tricycle. It's hard to keep this up because she is severely hung over.

She knows how to swing around the potholes without even looking, on her way into Lakewood. Hers is one of those that puts the garden in these garden apartments: ground floor with a cement patio out back, and a strip of grass between her patio and the next, the strips merging into a lumpy lawn down to the wall of concrete sound barrier panels separating the apartments from the interstate. The freeway screams past all day and night, but on this side of the wall the sound is just a low hum that rises and falls like breathing.

She turns on the TV, goes to the bathroom to pee, then takes Justin outside so he can play and she can sit in her plastic chair and smoke a cigarette. She slumps in the chair, closes her eyes. Her cigarette drops to the concrete pad where it burns to ash. "You tell that doctor he's crazy!" her mother had said. Maria shooed Justin into the car so that he wouldn't hear, but he heard it anyway. "That child needs some kind of medicine!" her mother said, and Maria said, "Don't talk that way in front of him," but there *she* was too, talking that way in front of him.

Her elbow slips and she goes sideways in the chair, and her dark curls fall over her face. She scratches her cheek with a long red fingernail, unconsciously careful not to rub away her foundation and blush, though it is makeup left over from the night before.

At least Justin's doctor wasn't mean (he wasn't really nice but he wasn't mean). The other one, the gynecologist, was an asshole ("groin-ecologist" she likes to call him). She remembers how he accused her: *multiple sex partners*, he said, just like that, real matter of fact, what the hell did he know? She had never in her life had "multiple sex partners"—like what, a bunch of bananas joined at the neck?—and she wanted to tell him that but she felt the corners of her mouth starting to tremble. She never had multiple sex partners, only one at a time, including Robbie, and now she wasn't sure about Robbie anymore, but she supposed the groin-ecologist wouldn't want to hear about *that*. And then there was Justin, the problem with her baby, baby Justin, coming back to her the way it always did, hurting in that terrible way, first, and then just worrying, worrying. Three years old, four next week. Justin didn't talk.

She shifts in her chair, and lifts a mascara-laden eyelid enough to locate her child, then shuts her eye again. The image of him lingers there, floats around behind her eyelids: plump and white and upright, sitting in the grass with his back to her, as if he is just staring into the tall barrier wall.

Justin hears the television behind him, in the living room, through the open patio door. Before he came outside, he'd sat on the rug and watched TV, while his mother was in the bathroom. Someone fell off a boat and was eaten by piranhas. The water looked like maybe it was tickling him all over, although Justin couldn't tell because the man was under the water, and then someone said that the piranhas were eating him, and then he knew the water wasn't tickling. Maybe if you were underwater you could see the man and see the piranhas and what was happening, but above the water all you could see was the top of the water, popping all over like popcorn in the microwave—which you couldn't see either until it was finished and you could open the bag. You could not see what was going on inside the bag but you could hear it. Popcorn was noisy. But the piranhas did not make any noise.

The man never came out of the water again. Maybe that meant everything got eaten, bones and everything, like a donut or a candy bar, not like a chicken leg where you don't eat the bone, or an egg where you don't eat the shell. His mother let him hold an egg once, she said it was hard-boiled so it was okay to hold. The outside was smooth and just like the piranhas you couldn't see what was underneath, but, unlike the piranhas, which just showed on top, the egg went all the way around. He didn't know what hard-boiled meant. He could not tell by looking at it, or by holding it and shaking it. He wanted to smack it but he was afraid to, not knowing what would happen to the egg and then what would happen to him afterwards. All these secrets were hiding inside the egg.

Then there was a man who stepped in quicksand. He looked down and his feet were sinking, and then his legs. He was disappearing. It was scarier than piranhas because you could see the man, see the parts of him that hadn't disappeared yet. Once a part of you was down in there you couldn't get it back out except maybe a little bit, like an arm that might go down in there and then come up looking all wet with the sleeve sticking to it and stuff like oatmeal all over it which was the quicksand. But big parts, like your stomach and legs, never could come out again. It reminded him of bubblebath, the way you can't see your body underneath but you know it's there, but bubblebath you can get out of. There's no way to see under bubblebath. You can only see it from on top. In that way it's like piranhas.

The more you struggled in quicksand, the more quickly you sank. If you did not struggle, you sank more slowly. So which was worse?

He hoped there wasn't any quicksand out in the yard. He would not go very far in case there was. He worried about puddles that were left after rainstorms, maybe they had piranhas under them. You couldn't see through them, what you saw were the reflections of things—clouds, birds, your face. But they were just water, and when you had water in a glass you could see through it, it was the only thing that didn't have any color. In the bathtub you could see through it (unless you made a bubblebath), in the toilet you could see it and the toilet is deeper than a puddle.

There are no puddles around right now—he knows the places where they appear—and that is good. He hears men yelling on the TV. Somebody screams *Hold your fire!* and Justin makes a face. He cups his hands together and looks into them. The only thing he knows about fire is that it is very hot and it burns you if you touch it. What are the men on TV doing? He doesn't want to know. It's scary, like quicksand and piranhas.

He stares at the big wall.

Maria rolls her eyes, but her eyes are closed. The only thing keeping her from falling asleep is that her neck hurts at this angle. The cigarette is dead on the concrete.

She thinks of her mother—how just because she keeps Justin overnight once or twice a week she thinks she owns him or something.

She thinks of the groin-ecologist again. After he did the procedure to fix her cervix, she got up the courage to ask why this had happened to her. *Risk factors,* the doctor said. That's when he said, *multiple sex partners.* He said that she probably couldn't have more children. Probably, what did probably mean? She asked him if it meant she could stop taking birth control pills. *It means nothing of the sort,* he said, snorting at her.

She hasn't told Robbie about all that. Lately her love life is wound up tight as a—tight as a what? Maria is starved for similes. Tight as the skins on the drum set Robbie wishes he could play instead of the bass guitar that he learned to play last year so he could join his buddy's country music band. "Wow," she told him, "I never knew a musician before." "I ain't no musician," he said, but she noticed he wore a bass guitar belt buckle.

He hangs his thumbs on that buckle, and strokes his fingers over it sometimes in an absent-minded way that is like he is actually strumming it. He walked into the bar last night like that, thumbs in buckle. He was late and she'd been sitting there by herself a while, had thought to order him a Jack Daniels but then held off, went ahead and got a beer for herself, and a lady's drink, a shot of tequila—she liked whiskey but didn't drink it in bars. It was noisy and smoky in there, lots of laughter and pool balls cracking, and a jukebox across the room that thumped so much she couldn't make out the songs.

Some guy who'd given up losing money at pool came over and asked who the beer was for, and then when he got the answer he was expecting asked who the shot was for, and then when he got the answer to that he asked one more question which he had to lean down and breathe in her ear to ask. She told him what he could do with his question (fucking smart ass), and he said, "Hey, honey, I don't mean nothing by it."

"Well go do it someplace else. I'm waiting for somebody."

"You don't have to get upset."

He positioned himself two barstools down, where a friend of his, another down on his luck world-class champion pool player, joined him.

She could hear them talking about her, saw the looks they sent her way and then shared back and forth, that were meant for her to see and not meant for her to see at the same time. She bought herself another drink before they got the chance to think up buying one for her, though as she fumbled for matches and noted neither one of them reaching for a light, she realized she didn't need to worry.

Robbie walked in and sat down next to her, but did not notice her two admirers. They never stopped their foolishness—pretending to fall off their barstools when they looked at her, then recovering themselves, and then looking again and pretending to fall down again. It bothered her to see Robbie not even noticing men noticing her. Men never see fucking anything, she thought. Then he finished his bourbon and pushed the glass away, and he leaned into

Maria's ear and whispered. He said it might be different if all those guys checkin' out girls the way they do looked maybe like fuckin' movie stars themselves, but they don't. He grinned at her, and she felt proud and satisfied and appreciated. But then out of the corner of her eye she thought she saw his smile turning to a leer and his eyes moving down to her ass, and she looked up sharply, in time to catch him winking at the two guys down the bar.

He was smart enough to know when he'd been caught. He said, "Hey hey hey Maria, baby, *I* look like a movie star, don't I?" And she inspected him, as ruthlessly as any man had ever inspected her—the tight blue jeans, big boots, little beer gut, scraggly hair, pretty-boy smile.

"You're a movie star all right. A fuckin' rock star."

And she was still looking, and it was turning him on. He wasn't bad-looking—he was what they would have called, back in high school, cute.

"Yeah, you're cute," she said.

"Cute? Cute nothin'. Cute is for teddy bears, and I ain't no bear."

He was more than half drunk.

"I'm a tiger, a tiger for you, Maria, I'm your tiger, baby, I'm your tiger-baby, baby, baby Maria."

Now he was showing off, showing her off, in front of these people they didn't know, and she thought she liked that but wasn't sure.

Later, out in the parking lot, leaning back with his butt on the hood of her old Malibu, he held her close to him and murmured her name in her ear, over and over, with a softness that exactly fitted her hearing, their closeness, and it felt nice to hear her name that way, as if he was telling her, I'm thinking of you, of you, of you.

She thinks she should get up and go inside but can't. She thinks she should get something to eat but doesn't think she can eat. Justin is already fed, he had Spaghettios at her mom's, it had made her half sick to see those things in the bowl and smell them but she sat with him on the floor there while he ate and watched TV. "Look at the man talking on the telephone, look at his funny hair." She said it because she always talked to him but also because the character on the TV was describing a sex act, and she didn't know if Justin would understand but thought she should distract him. Then a commercial came on, and those were always easier to talk about. "Look at that shiny floor, it looks so pretty, what are those kids singing about, oh look they're going to eat now, I think they're eating noodles like you are." Her mother came out of the kitchen and stared at her as if she wished she would leave, or wanted her to do something she wasn't doing, and Maria wanted to say, What the hell's your problem? but not in front of Justin. She went back to studying the television. "Look at the buildings," she said. It was hard to keep up these one-way conversations.

Last night, on the way home from the bar, she got a flat tire. She should have just gone to Robbie's in the first place, he wanted her to—it's Saturday night, he kept saying, and Justin's at your mom's—but she couldn't explain to him why she wouldn't go. Maybe it was fate, but she was scared to think that way.

She heard a thump-thump-thump, and at first thought she had run over an animal. She was only a block from the turn back into her apartment complex and felt mad that it happened right there, out under the big streetlights. Right across the road there was a disgusting-looking mattress that had fallen off someone's car, which was half in the street and half on the sidewalk.

She was irritated that she had to walk to her apartment, so she stayed and smoked a cigarette first. She had no idea how to change a tire, it just wasn't the kind of thing she would ever do. She was grinding out the butt with her heel and staring into the back of one of the apartment buildings when a puttputt-sounding little sedan pulled over behind her. Its turn signal was on, blinking faster than most, too fast she thought, and she was apprehensive and thought this was a weird little car, and then the man got out and he seemed a lot like the car, and it didn't make her feel any better.

His name was Ferdinand. He introduced himself politely, as if maybe they were meeting at a fancy cocktail party rather than on the side of an empty highway at two in the morning. She felt nervous. She noticed the tassels on his shiny loafers, and bits of glass glittering around them in the road. It made her think of *Cinderella* or the *Wizard of Oz* or something. She looked up when he took a step back. He was rubbing his hands together and saying, "Let me get right to changing your tire for you."

She felt better about him then, and besides she was still a little buzzed from the bar, and curious, so she followed him to the trunk of his car and watched him. He was bent over, looking for something, and humming to himself. He had a cute butt, she thought, sort of visible through the fabric of his suit pants. The sleeves of his white shirt were folded back neatly just above the wrists. He came up with a stack of rags, which he started wiping his hands on even though he hadn't touched her flat tire yet. He wasn't bad-looking, but he was plain. She liked his hair which was short and neat but still looked casual and fluffy. Before he closed his trunk she saw how he had matching luggage in there. She never knew anybody with luggage, real matching suitcases.

He was pretty quiet, so she started talking while he was changing her tire. She told him how she'd actually had the tires longer than she'd had the car. Really, she said, believe it or not, this car came without tires and so she had to put the tires from her Impala on the Malibu and sell the Impala without tires, which wasn't easy, she had to sell it cheap, but that was okay because she got the Malibu cheap because it also did not have tires. Crazy, huh? she asked him. He grunted in a way that sounded disapproving but then she saw that it was just the sound he made pulling off the old tire. He rolled it away and leaned it against her fender, and rolled the spare to where he wanted it. She noticed how careful he was not to get anything on his clothes.

"What do you do?" she asked, because he was being so quiet.

"I'm in sales," he said.

"Are you a traveling salesman?"

He laughed. "I guess so. I do have to travel a lot."

Maybe he didn't want to talk about it, about what he sold for a living, she thought, because it was something embarrassing, like tampons or something, or maybe he didn't want to talk about it because he had to talk about it all the time when he was working. Or maybe he didn't want to talk to *her*—this girl with tangled hair who smelled like a bar. But he looked up at her then and smiled and said, "I think she's ready to go."

Maria thought it cute the way he called her car a *she* and wanted to say so, but then thought that maybe it was a totally normal thing to him to talk like that and she didn't want to put her foot in her mouth.

He was wiping his hands on the rags from his trunk. He was the kind of man who carried a supply of nice, clean rags.

She had never known anybody named Ferdinand, and suddenly wanted to say that too but didn't. In fact she had never known anyone with a name anything *like* Ferdinand, which sounded so funny to her as she said it to herself in her mind. He was putting the tools away in the back of her car; it was taking a while because he was organizing her trunk. She watched as he shifted things around, a broken umbrella, an old shoebox, empty soda cans. He settled everything with great care, as if each was a precious thing, and it nearly broke her heart to see. She wanted to say, you don't have to do that, it's all trash, it doesn't matter, but she didn't because she couldn't bear for him to think it didn't matter if he was so sure, for some reason, it did. He held up a teddy bear with a torn armpit and began poking the stuffing back into him. Oh gosh, she wanted to say, that's just an old, messed-up bear, it's my little boy's—

"I have a little boy," she said.

"I know," he said, pointing to a pair of small sneakers he had found in opposite corners of the trunk and had placed side by side.

It was two o'clock in the morning and a stranger with a funny name was fixing her son's teddy bear on the side of the road.

Ferdinand's eyebrows were screwed up in concentration, his face bright under the streetlight, poking at the bear's armpit.

"My little boy—" she said but caught her breath, seeing Ferdinand settle the bear in a nest he'd made of the rags (his own rags, he was leaving them). He patted the bear's tummy and smiled to himself, and she would have given anything to know his thoughts, and she remembered again how bizarre this all was, and she thought suddenly that maybe he was making fun of her.

"Your little boy?" he asked, closing the lid of the trunk, looking at her, still smiling. His eyes were kind.

"Yes," she said. But she couldn't say anything else, he stood there waiting but she couldn't, because of what he'd done, because of the way he'd arranged everything so perfectly in her trunk.

He began stepping back toward his car, and he nodded sweetly to her but she knew he had to think she was acting strange. He tipped an imaginary hat to her, like someone in a movie.

"He's—he's a good boy," she managed to say. He nodded, waved as he neared his car, turned away. He wore a white tee shirt under his shirt, even in summer, she saw. He was that kind of person.

"Thank you," she called out, remembering her manners.

And then, even though she was less than half a mile from her own door, she turned around and went to Robbie's, she didn't know why.

When he wouldn't wake up and come to the door she had to drive to the convenience store and wait her turn to use the payphone. She hated this but she had accidentally dropped her cell phone into the river off the Pleasant Road bridge two weeks before, Robbie's fault because he was goofing around and made her drop it while they were walking across the bridge to his friend's house. She was going to get a new one but just hadn't done it yet.

A fat man with a scary beard was on the payphone, arguing with someone, and Maria sat with her car running, trying not to stare at him. She sat crouched down behind her steering wheel, shooting beady-eyed glances at everyone who pulled up. The guys got out of their cars but the girls waited behind, smoking and looking bored. There were fast, nervous guys who dashed into the store (crank-heads, thought Maria), and slow ones, who got out of their cars and stood there, getting themselves together before they commenced walking (drunks, thought Maria). At this time of night, no one was buying anything wholesome. They were coming out with cigarettes and yesterday's donuts and nasty things like beef jerky.

No one looked twice at Maria, although everyone looked once, and some of the guys looked a little longer than they might have, and ran their eyes over her car as if it were her body, lingering on her rear end.

There were no Ferdinands there. Ferdinand would never know what that was like, screeching into the 7-11 desperate for a pack of cigarettes in the middle of the night. That much she knew about him. Wherever he was going at two o'clock in the morning, he wasn't stopping there. Maybe in the middle of the day, though: standing in line with the construction workers and the mothers with their kids, a quart of milk under his arm, coming and going almost invisible, disappearing in his puttputt car.

When she finally got to use the phone, she cupped her hands around the receiver while it rang and rang and watched as a skinny guy with long, matted hair got out of his car, stood in the space between his car and hers, and flicked his cigarette ash through her open window onto the seat, as if her car were some big ashtray. He kept standing there, looking around—he seemed to have no idea where he was—and then did it again, without looking, without seeing, flicked his ash through her window.

"Robbie, Robbie!" she said when he finally answered.

"What's wrong?"

"I want to come over, I have to get out of here."

"Out of where?"

Backing out, she ran one wheel over the curb, and something underneath her car scraped, making a metal-against-concrete sound. The streets were black, damp-looking, the streetlights over them pink, with haloes. The left turns and right turns were like a ritual, the slowing, the speeding up, the slowing again. She thought how her spare tire was on the car now, which meant she had no spare.

He'd left the door open for her but was asleep when she got there, rolled on his side facing the wall, musty-smelling and naked under a balled-up sheet. She was losing her alcohol buzz and the headache and dryness were filling in, but Robbie always kept Tylenol and aspirin and water by his bed—this was funny since everything else about him was a mess, always a mountain of dishes in the sink, always losing his bills in piles of junk mail—but he always had painkillers and enough water for both of them right in reach. She helped herself to these and got undressed.

"Robbie, wake up."

"No."

"Wake up, come on, be nice." She wiggled the length of her body against his back. "Robbie, Robbie, honey—"

"What the, what the fuck, cut it out!" He pushed her back, and punched his pillow. He curled up tighter against the wall.

"Fuck you," said Maria.

She rolled onto her back and blinked at the dark ceiling. She let herself think about Ferdinand. The whole thing seemed like a dream. Now that it was over there was an empty feeling about it, as if she had missed a chance to say something, to make something clear. Not that she knew what it was. At least she didn't say anything stupid, which was better. Better not to say anything about something you didn't understand.

She hadn't told him about herself, and he may have got the wrong impression. But what was there to know? What was there to say? I'm the girl who works at the supermarket bakery, who writes Happy Birthday on the cakes, I drive around on bald tires and party on the weekends, I live in a piece of shit one-bedroom apartment with my little boy who can't talk.

But Robbie knew all that and he didn't care, they didn't even have to discuss it. Which was good, she supposed. Maybe it meant that he loved her. And he had rescued her from the convenience store. Saved her from spending the night alone. But then she looked hard at the ceiling—she had been rescued to sleep here in this saggy bed next to this smelly, snoring man.

In the morning she got up, found her clothes, saw her lipstick smeared on the pillowcase. She left there without disturbing Robbie, without a word.

◆ ◆ ◆

Justin, sitting on the grass, twists his body around to get a look at his mother. She is sleeping, he thinks, she must be tired. He would like to go crawl up her lap, but he is afraid to wake her up. If he wakes her she might get mad. She is the most beautiful person he knows, but if she wakes up angry she may turn into an ugly person. He has seen this happen, and it's very frightening, not because the ugliness is so ugly (although it is) but because the change is so sudden. He has heard her say, stop crying! why are you crying?! which just makes him cry more, which makes her madder, which makes her uglier, which makes him cry and cry. But it doesn't happen very often.

And right now she is beautiful, and Justin thinks, hopes, this is his *real* mommy. It can't possibly be that she is both beautiful and ugly, only one can really be real, and he has to believe it's the beautiful mother who is real. She has lovely milky skin that he likes to push his nose into. She has shiny pretty lips and her teeth are the same way. She has beautiful ears and sometimes they play whispery games and he tickles her ear and then she tickles his ear. Her sweater has little funny nubbies all over. Her hair is like a princess's hair. She has different smells and all of them are good; there is the scent of her hair, her lipstick. The smell of her neck which is no smell but it's the best of all.

Justin hears the television again. The commercials are always louder than the shows. The TV says this is the color you've always dreamed of for your hair, and now you can have it. You've tried other colors, but this is your real color. Justin thinks of his mother's long black, bouncy hair. Then the television says, this is the color lips crave, if lips could talk, this is the color they would ask for. Justin tries to imagine TV lips that *don't* talk, lips that just sit there like large waxy objects. Then he looks up at his mother's mouth, notes that it does not move, sees the glossy red lips so bright against the white skin, the black hair; sees her lips are parted, just a little, as if to speak but they don't speak; he can't see her teeth behind the dark opening, it is as if her teeth are not even there, as if her mouth is a cave. He turns away quickly, looks at the wall again. It never changes, never moves, always makes the same sound, like a low, important whispering, too rumbly and run together to make out the words if there are any, only now he can't hear it because the TV is still blaring.

Maria tries to sit up a little in her chair, tries to think, but it's hard because she feels like hell.

She understands what the doctor meant about the birth control. She understood even at the time. She's not stupid. He meant that she couldn't carry a baby although she could still get pregnant. And she heard and understood the words he said, like *possible hysterectomy*. She remembers how he stood by the door with his hand on the doorknob and his other hand sunk in a fist in the pocket of his starched white labcoat. He wanted her out of there.

Justin's doctor is different. He is cool and professional, and the way he talks makes her want to try to be a better mom. She can't say that to him, though, instead pretends she already is a good mom.

He said Justin's speech was *developing more slowly*. He said for some children *it is slower*. But she could hear the word *slow* inside his words. He told her not to worry, and that the problem with him was not her fault. She has told her mother a million times what the doctor said, but it's as if she doesn't even hear.

What if her mother is right?

Maybe she should ask Robbie what he thinks. But she knows he won't have anything to say.

What would Ferdinand think? But that's a stupid question, because she'll never see Ferdinand again.

Ferdinand would understand. She imagines the soothing sound of his voice, talking about Justin. She hears him, too, talking about her, saying he understands about the gynecologist.

Ferdinand is gone. There are no Ferdinands, not in her world.

Ferdinand would make a good dad for Justin—another crazy thought! But she can't imagine having sex with Ferdinand. Robbie is her kind of guy. This is just a fact. This is reality.

What kind of dad would Robbie be?

If she knew Robbie better, she might not love him.

This is a weird thought. She sits up a little, blinks her eyes open, sees the back of her son's head.

Then she wonders, would it make any difference, would it change anything, if I knew him better? If I didn't love him? If he was somebody else? Some other half-employed, half-assed thinks-he-can-play-the-bass-guitar redneck drunk, which is what he would still be if he was somebody else?

Justin looks at the wall. It is so large, but he does not know what it is. It has always been there. It is the only wall he knows. His grandma does not have one. No one else has one.

It makes a sound, all the time, as if it's trying to tell him something. He can see how tall it is, and how it goes on and on in both directions. The one thing he can't tell about it is its depth. For all he knows the wall is thick, so thick it goes forever and ever.

It doesn't frighten him. It is always there where he expects it and it does not move. It doesn't attack you like piranhas or suck you under, into nothing, like quicksand. Quicksand you can never get out of. The only way is if somebody else pulls your arms.

He can't figure out the wall, what it means, what it's for. Maybe when he is bigger he will be able to understand it.

Maybe—even better—maybe when he is old enough, his mother will explain it to him. She knows everything.

He feels himself being picked up under the armpits, and he doesn't startle, doesn't turn or make a noise because it's one of the familiar feelings in his world—the pressure of his mother's hands, together with the smell of her and the sound of her breathing behind his neck. He goes limp, waiting for the next expected thing, to feel himself lifting up and turning, and then his feet are leaving the ground—he looks down and sees his toes pointing at the grass. Their arms bump and his clothes pull as his shirt rubs against hers, and he is being twisted to face her, and her arms are tight around him and he wraps his arms around her neck. She presses her cheek against his, and she smells beautiful, like flowers. Her hair slips over his eye like a shade, and he likes that, it makes him feel as if he's hiding. He is smiling, but then he feels wet on his cheek, from her cheek. Her tears run into his mouth. She doesn't make a sound. Why? he wants to ask her. Why are you crying? He knows you can cry without making any noise, that part he understands and he wants her to know that, and so he holds on to her just as tight as anybody ever could, and he is sure she knows. She knows, doesn't she know?

But she is crying a lot now, why is she crying? All he can do is hug her tighter and tighter.

But now she loosens her arms a little. This is the best kind of hug—not too hard, not too soft. Her tears are stopping. She starts rocking him. She is doing a little dance, stepping side to side. He smiles, throws his head back, squeezes his eyes shut. Crying doesn't matter, he thinks. It washes out your eyes! And he is glad that the hugging is lasting longer than the crying.

He giggles, a tiny escaping music, but unmistakable, the ringing of a bell, and his mother looks at him and laughs, herself, to encourage him to try to do it again.

Something, Anything

My wife is one of these people who drives on the freeway with a mattress on top of her car, held there by a single string.

I first found her in a duplex made over into apartments, on a street of duplexes in Arbutus, Maryland, on the edge of Baltimore. Red-and-white petunias were a popular choice for window boxes up and down the street, and overly frilly curtains for the windows. Parking was tight because there were no driveways, and the front lawns were tiny, some of them replaced by miniature fields of ornamental stone.

When she asked me, I told her I was unattached. She said that she was semi-detached, like a dwelling. Like a duplex, I said, and that's when she pointed out that all along the street the duplexes had been turned into apartments: each half-a-building had one up, one down. So no, not like a duplex, she said. It was the first instance of my not being able to follow what the hell she was talking about. But then, the way she always does, she added something that made sense. She said she rented there because she was convinced the duplex building didn't look like apartments, but just like two real homes.

She slows down because of that mattress on top of her car, by doing 70 instead of 80.

The latest thing with her is she won't go to Taco Bell since they retired the chihuahua. (Good riddance, I say, because I can't believe she would go there at all, though I don't know if it's better or worse that she only went there because of that dog.) And she won't go to shopping malls at all, even at Christmas, because she says they're not natural. (As if a dog selling burritos is.)

I laugh and say, I have grown richer while you have grown stranger, and it's just a joke but she doesn't seem to appreciate it. It's not even true—I've made money but she has been just this strange all along. And in fact I've always known it, from the moment I fell in love with her, which was not on the stoop of her duplex but later, in the winter, after a snowstorm, when her heat went out and I found the door open—why not? she said, it isn't like I need to keep out the cold, and besides, that way I didn't have to get out from under the covers to let you in—that's how I found her, curled up in a ball in the bed, trying not to move and spill the inch of heat around her edge, cold as a tit on a witch. She looked at me and said, your lips are too blue to kiss. It wasn't true, I was as warm as could be, she was the one who was cold, she was just projecting. I felt sorry for her, saying things like that. And then she told me how she'd got there while it was still snowing and found she had locked herself out of the house, so then she was digging for the spare key in the snow, turning over flowerpots, snow blowing all around her head. It's another reason to leave the door ajar, she said. What do you mean? I said. Because it was too-locked earlier, now it is very unlocked and I want it that way, the two will balance each other out. It made no sense at all. Then she said: but I am so glad you're here now. And that made sense, which made it possible for me to fall in love with her at that moment. I swear to you my motives were as pure as they have ever been before or since.

Every time I close my eyes, all I see is that damn mattress. I have never been able to understand why nobody thinks to tie those things fore-and-aft. Think for one blessed moment where the wind comes from, when you're driving forward in a straight line on a freeway.

She is, I have to say, despite anything else she is, a useful person. She has always been good to take to functions because she is still strikingly attractive and very social, more social than I, the hit of the party because she is so quirky. My friends' wives say I am remarkably attentive to her. We look good together in public.

Your wife is a card, they say. Which one? I ask, the Queen of Diamonds? The Joker? At one of these parties she managed to find a lampshade—a small one from one of those lamps that looks like a candle, the kind you put in a window—and she set it atop her head for a joke, the old joke where you get drunk at a party and ending up wearing a lampshade—except it was just a tiny lampshade wobbling on top of her big, puffy, copper or bronze hair (which one it is I don't know, we have argued about this, all I know is it's metallic), and she was completely sober, too. Ha ha ha, making a complete ass of herself still sitting around the dinner table with all those competing perfumes and everyone in their nicest clothes and the leg of lamb and the good cabernet.

I let her drive home. I'd had quite a bit to drink. She's telling me in the car how she loves to be in the rocking chair. The what? She says that's what the tractor trailer drivers call it, when you're in the middle, some space in front and behind you but some trucks up ahead and back there—see them? Sure enough I see them, their tail lights, like a red, shifting constellation, rolling ahead, far ahead of us, sure I see them but they're a little blurred together for me. And I look at her looking in the rearview mirror, at the trucks behind us in the distance, her face glowing in that light that comes from somewhere in cars in the dark, and she has this fragile smile on her face just thinking of it: rocking in the rocking chair, driving with the trucks.

And I wonder if she's trying that now, with the mattress I mean. It might be good to keep a little distance with that thing on top of the car. They will probably give her a wide berth. They should. But they don't know her like I do. They better give that woman some space.

The Queen of Hearts stole some tarts, I remember thinking. In fact, I said it out loud, there in the car. The Deuce is wild, I said. Are you drunk? she said, laughing. You only loosen up when you drink, she said, it's too bad. It's too bad, because if you... I tipped my seat back at that point. She's the one who had put the lampshade on her head—but maybe she'd forgotten about that. That's when she asked me what was the difference between eccentric and crazy. I just stared at the leather-crinkle texture of the car's headliner, and I couldn't tell how far it was from my face.

Then she asked me again, what's the difference between eccentric and crazy. I told her I couldn't say. That, evidently, was a problem, because she proceeded to tell me all about it. How crazy was dysfunctional but eccentric was just a way of coping with the world. I wasn't about to ask which one she was, but she turned to look at me with her mouth open like a bird wanting to be fed, as if to say, ask me, ask me.

And I waited to see what was the thing she would say that would make sense. But it never came. Keep your eyes on the highway, I requested.

What are you? she said.

What do you mean? I said.

Are you one or the other? Eccentric or crazy?

What do you think? I answered. I was not about to go down that road with her, you know what I'm saying?

She said, I think *you* don't think you're either one—
—That's right.
—but I think you're a little strange yourself.

So, as I said, I kept waiting for the thing that made sense. What I couldn't figure out was why we were talking about me and not her in this context. I was sobering up. I gave her a long, close look—there have been times in my marriage when I felt I didn't know this person at all and needed to refamiliarize myself, and this was one of them. Her eyes were clear and dark—nothing like the girl curled in the cold in her duplex apartment with the door open. For a minute I thought I loved her more this way. It scared me, frankly.

Which one are you, she said again, eccentric or crazy? In a breathy voice like a movie star or an asthmatic.

What happens if I don't want to answer this question?

Why don't you want to answer it?

Can we talk about something else?

Why don't you ask *me* something?

What the hell would I ask you?

Isn't there something you want to ask, something, anything?

Why are we talking in all these questions?

Why can't you answer me?

Is this like a game? To see who slips and runs out of questions first?

Why can't you talk to me?

Can we just drop this?

I watched her loading stuff into that little U-Haul trailer. I stood there in the driveway, with a cup of coffee in my hand—you can never get enough caffeine. I asked her, what would you do if that mattress flew off the top of your car? It's the fantasy you always have, when you see those people on the highway with the forward half of their mattress flapping up and down. You wonder if they feel it at all, some vibration or a kind of rhythmic hesitation, caused by wind resistance. You wonder what it would look like in one of those wind tunnels, with the colored streams of wind—the turbulence.

I say to her: I repeat, what would you do if that mattress flew off your car?

She didn't answer. It's this thing with the questions again, I guess. Still mad about that. But at least now I'm asking her something. Isn't that what she wanted?

I know the answer anyway, I think. She's reached a point in her life where she's the kind of person who wouldn't stop and go back and get it. She'd reflexively lift her foot from the gas when she felt it happen, but then reapply her foot and just plow on.

She looked at me before she got in the car. She'd declined my offer of a moving company, out of spite. Perhaps not out of spite.

I held my hands out, palms up, supplicant. She held her hands out in turn, and opened them, as if tossing petals into the air. She shook her head, but slowly, not the little-kid no-no-no way she usually does, but looking at me the whole time, her eyes shining that dark way, and then she smiled. It was that fragile smile, that rearview-mirror smile, that rocking-chair smile.

With any luck, the string will hold. Amazingly, it seems to, when you see those people going down the road.

I hold to that, then. A disturbing image but not disastrous. Before I even close my eyes, I know what I'll see. My wife in the car which she deserved but which I bought her, crazy mattress waving bye-bye.

The Detectorist

He had been walking in the highway median for two hours, but he still hadn't seen all of it. It was a big one, long and wide with a spine of trees down the middle that hid the cars on either side from each other's view, but while they might not see each other, some of them did see him, a sudden, static figure, glimpsed and gone.

The people in the cars had a moment of surprise, then suspicion, then dismissal: he looked middle-aged and soft, dressed in overalls, slouched in the round-shouldered posture of a primate at the zoo. And the shape of the thing he held—the metal tube that pointed at the ground, with something, a dark shape, at the bottom—this registered in the drivers' memories as distantly familiar. So they put him in that category of people you see by the side of the road who are doing God-knows-what but it doesn't matter because you'll never know, and they kept their eyes on the long sweep of the highway ahead of them, past woods and old Virginia farmland quilted with subdivisions.

He was doing fine until he happened to step over a log and look to his left, into the trees, and he saw it—it wasn't the color that caught his attention, blending with the dirt and sticks and leaves, or its texture, which was dull, or its size, which was no bigger than the proverbial breadbox, but the fact that it was squirming so much.

It was not a wounded deer, nothing like that. It was not human—he was relieved to realize it was too small for that, unless it was . . . a baby? But no, he stared at it, observing the constant movement all over it—not a baby.

He had the strangest feeling that he knew what it was but couldn't name it, and he started to perspire.

He removed his headphones and set his metal detector on the ground and walked into the trees, the sound of his boots in the dry leaves a colossal crunching in his ears and the whine of the passing cars suddenly high-pitched, loud. But these sounds disappeared as his eyes and nose started to run and he began making the gasping, catching, squeaking noises of someone trying to resist terrible, inevitable sneezing. He stopped, backed up, and sneezed half a dozen times, then sneezed some more.

A moment earlier, he'd been thinking about something he found from the Battle of Chancellorsville, an eagle hat plate, also called a Hardee hat plate—made of thin stamped brass, featuring an eagle with outstretched wings, three arrows in its left claw, an olive branch in its right, *e pluribus unum* on a banner in its beak, and thirteen clouds above its head standing for the original thirteen colonies. The plate had been worn, he knew, on the hat of a Union cavalryman.

A moment before that, he had been noting the tint in the trees, which meant a time was coming when it would be too cold to do this, the ground would be frozen and he would not be able to dig.

Before that, for some reason, he had been thinking of the name his parents gave him. He had been born on Christmas Eve, and the name Noelle was already taken by the twin sister who preceded him into the world by five minutes. His mother once claimed she almost named them Noelle and Noel but saw the absurdity of this and so she called her son Rudolph. He went by Rudy, having found it was sometimes possible to cover up what was preposterous in life by altering its appearance.

But now he was sneezing his ass off and holding his head with both hands and the oaks and poplars were swimming before his eyes as tears streamed down his cheeks, and he knew exactly why.

He staggered backwards, like a charging drunk in reverse. The sneezing eased. He sat down on the log he'd stepped over a moment before.

So. They were kittens. He couldn't see them now, from where he was. What would he do? He could take them home except for one problem and it wasn't his allergies, and it wasn't his girlfriend's allergies which were even worse than his, it was his girlfriend's personality, which was not compatible with the idea of homeless kittens and the symptoms they triggered.

Their allergies were how they'd met—Lydia had the 10:15 appointment at the allergist on Fridays while Rudy had the 10:30, and since the place ran late, she was always there when he arrived, and they had to sit and wait before they went in for their allergy shots. It was weeks before they spoke, and when they did Rudy learned that Lydia was about to give up because the shots didn't seem to be helping, so he worked up the courage a week later to ask her out, afraid he might not otherwise see her again.

Lydia would be outraged if he brought home kittens. Lydia was a very assertive woman. He still wasn't sure what she saw in him, and after four months of living together—still a shock to him to think she had wanted to, although she had been laid off from her job with a telecommunications company and this had something to do with it—after four months he felt sure that a fairly small thing, nothing as big as a bag full of kittens, was all it would take to put an unhappy end to the experiment.

He could drive them to the animal shelter—not even take them out of the bag—but the thought of going near that place, with all those *cats!* Maybe he could just call them, tell them where to find the kittens, and they would send out a patrol? But that was a coward's way out. The picture of that squirming sack of kittens kept coming back to him—how long had they been there? Someone must have carried or thrown them pretty far for them to be all the way up in the edge of the trees. Were they hurt? Were they all alive in there?

Lydia would tell him to forget it. Get out of there, call your friends, see if they want to mess with it. She always argued from logic. So why was this killing him like this?

Maybe he could take them to his father's place. His father—who spent his days at the big book store near his home in Manassas, drinking coffee and walking around talking to anyone who would listen about his favorite subjects: the economy, the Bible, and the War of Northern Aggression. The idea of a half dozen kittens in that crazy old man's tiny apartment made Rudy shake his head and give it up as soon as he thought of it.

He was not sure to this day how he felt about his father's rabid confederacy. Growing up, because of his father's outspoken views, Rudy had taken a neutral stand in the War Between the States. In his metal detecting, what he was after in digging up bullets and buttons and belt buckles was a glimpse into what it had felt like, North or South, it didn't matter. When Rudy dug something up from the ground—catching the signal, the beep or bonk in his headphones, and narrowing on it, listening carefully, trying to distinguish good brass from junk, and then loosening the earth with his shovel and pulling it apart, carefully, with his hands, sifting it with his fingers—when his eye caught the flat plane of a breastplate, or the small mound of a brass button, he felt, every time, a kind of sliding away inside himself, a falling away of time just like the dirt falling away from the sudden, distinct, old muddy metal, and he was there with the man who had lost the button or thrown away the cracked badge, and he knew him, sensed him, felt the man's world pressing down around him.

Because Rudy did most of his detecting at the sites of army camps—which is what this grassy island dividing the highway was reputed to be—he mostly glimpsed the waiting and the boredom and the sitting still, not the intangible quality he knew he was after but could not name, some feeling that came to men in battle, some knowledge that came to them when they understood that they were, really, like it or not, soldiers.

He knew his father, if asked (and he sure wouldn't ask him), would lay claim to comprehending this elusive quality. His father, well into his eighties and forgetful of things like the month and the year, held maps of Gettysburg and Shiloh in his head. He had never been in the military himself, due to some problem with his legs, never clarified. He had, oddly, no interest at all in his son's metal detecting or the artifacts he found. Rudy had a clear, early memory of his father standing tall and still, for once in his life with nothing to say, staring out over the bloody cornfield at Antietam. He had tears in his eyes, which was why the memory had stuck.

And Rudy's mother, she'd lay claim, if she were still alive, to knowing the heart of a soldier in battle. She could talk the talk when it came to Southern pride and Southern valor, but he had to remember that this was the woman who'd named her Christmas babies Noelle and Rudolph. The main problem with her was the way she revised history, for instance, when Rudy was eight or nine years old, up and claiming she was born in California instead of South Carolina as everybody knew she was. Or deciding, when Rudy was about fourteen, that her great-grandmother had been a slave on a tobacco plantation instead of the deep-rooted Anglo-Saxon white woman he'd been told about. Rudy thought, at first, the slave story was just to get a rise out of the old man, until she changed her story again, claiming that her great-grandmother had been a runaway nun from a Spanish convent. Rudy took refuge all his life in his mother's warm eccentricity, until her death five years ago, but he learned, at a tender age, that he had to trust his own version of events.

At the age of sixteen, standing in the study before the huge desk, before his father, who spent most of his free hours sitting there, staring out the window, Rudy had risked suggesting that the war had not been so glorious as all that, reminding his father that by war's end, one in four Southern men of soldiering age were dead. He said the war was savage and senseless, and his father snorted the word *senseless* out through his powerful nostrils, at which point Rudy brought up the subject of slavery, to which his father responded that the south hadn't been fighting about slavery, not one way or the other. "The war was about pride," the old man said, staring the boy down, his eyes narrowing to ferocious hardness, and it was not necessary to add *you must never forget this* or words to that effect. Rudy knew then that he was fighting a lost cause.

An hour later, he was summoned back to the study where his father informed him that, after much thought, he was prepared to overlook his son's insubordination, to forgive it as the youthful misjudgment of a junior officer. Rudy gave a toy-soldier salute, spun on his heel, and left the room. But he stole a look back before he disappeared, and this was what was most clear in memory—his father staring out the window, into some distant dream, a smile on his face that was smug yet innocent, a child's smile, a fragile, hopeful thing that made him look old and young at the same time and made Rudy wonder what was behind it, what his father was really trying, all the time, to be brave about.

He wondered again, now, what soldiers felt, as he sat on the log, and fingered the two bullets in his pocket—all he'd found so far—.58 caliber three-ring bullets, Union issue, nothing special. Never fired but simply dropped on the ground, after the gunpowder wrapped with them had been taken for starting campfires.

He remembered the kittens and felt ill. He thought of Lydia—Lydia had no use for the Civil War, or for metal detecting. On their second date he told her about it—he always blew it on the second date, usually for good, the exact same way, talking about metal detecting.

On his second date with Lydia, he thought to introduce her to his treasure hunting hobby through something more exotic than Civil War paraphernalia dug up in farm fields. He struck on the idea of a Spanish galleon, shipwrecked with a load of silver and gold, so he started to tell her about an article he'd read, about the breakup of the Montesserros off the coast of Mexico. She said, "Oh, the Montesserros, yeah it's so sad that they broke up," and he didn't get that she was making a joke. He explained, too stridently, what it was about. She got irritated. He told her how glass beads from the wreck would wash up on the beach all the time. She made a face. He thought she'd fall for the idea of jewelry—he said, "But wouldn't it be neat to find a lot of beads? Enough beads to make a bracelet?" to which she responded that she didn't want somebody else's beads, why would she want somebody else's beads?

Around that time, about a year ago, he had gone detecting one Friday after his allergy shots, took the rest of the day off and went to a farm near the Potomac that he knew. There had been a big camp there, parts of it used by both Union and Confederate forces at different times—Rudy always found something when he went, but that day he didn't find anything, and he ended up standing in one of the far fields, close enough to look in the windows of the new houses along the farm's edge. He thought how the Civil War camp continued underneath and past those houses, and wondered if the owners of those places had any idea, any idea at all, about what might still be buried under their new green lawns.

He studied the closest one: the columned Georgian doorway, the tall windows, the walls of blood-red brick. The twin heat pumps screened by shrubs, the big wrap-around deck. The split rail fence around the whole deal, to make clear where the field ended and the lawn began.

As he stood watching, a woman burst out onto the deck from the house, weeping and shrieking and swaying away from the door, then reeling and swinging back as if she would go inside, then turning away again. She was tall and thin and wore a long flesh-colored sheath that made her look spectral. She came to rest in the middle of the deck and stood sobbing and pressing her hands to her chest as if her breathing hurt. Rudy saw a side door onto the deck fly open and heard a man's voice yelling, although he could not see the man. The woman yelled back, in a wailing, forsaken voice, and kept crying, but never looked back to where the man was.

Rudy stood, motionless, the only vertical element in the middle of the bare dirt field, yet she did not see him—when she looked up, she stared past him, above him. There were long moments during which nothing was happening and then the man started yelling again, louder and angrier than before although Rudy couldn't make out the words. The woman started moving toward the open door, shaking her long arms at the man as if she were beating a big drum. She halted, and wailed, and took a step closer, and halted and wailed, and stepped closer, and then she was nearly at the door, and Rudy watched as the man's shape—his arms reaching—appeared from behind the door and wrenched her into the house. She screamed. The door slammed shut.

Rudy's hands were clammy and his mouth had dried up. He looked around—there was no one else there, no one but him. The other houses lay dormant while their owners were away at work. He looked down at his feet—a little bit of ground ivy the only green there against the reddish-brown earth, redder and browner if he kicked into it a little with his boots.

He waited till his heart slowed, and then he left, and went home and read metal detecting magazines.

As he sat there staring at the glossy pages, the question kept coming to him of what Lydia would have thought of him that day, and each time, he quickly flipped the page, to new ads, with new pictures, of shiny unmuddied metal detectors and compact folding shovels, pocket-knives, hats with stupid slogans.

The light was changing. The morning was turning to afternoon—how long had he been there? The kittens—God, he had to figure out what to do. He couldn't see them from where he was sitting—had they settled down some? He allowed himself the image of the knotted feed sack lying in the leaves motionless—all the kittens *dead* is what he meant—and he felt a wave of relief at this and then an immediate wave of shame at feeling that relief.

He told himself it didn't have to be as complicated as he was making it. He could call the animal shelter on his cell phone and ask them what to do. So why didn't he? Why not just do it? Why not?

He slapped his thighs in a decisive way and got up. He stood there, briefly dizzy, the tops of the trees stirring now in a light breeze and sunlight falling all around him, and the road below oddly empty of cars, and a crowd of starlings lifting, at that moment, from the woods on the other side of the highway.

He watched them rise, and school in the sky like fish, and move off, away south. He thought that the starlings were like those Union and Confederate boys, flown away from the earth, gone forever, all their memories with them. Nobodies of history, but I am a nobody too, he wanted to say to them. We are all of us historical accidents! He thought of his father's voice, intoning about the southland, talking about "our boys" as if they were still alive, not dead on the fields of war, and it occurred to him for the first time that his father, now that his hair and beard had grown white and wild, looked the very picture of a plantation owner though he was just a crazy old man people avoided in the bookstore. And Rudy thought of his mother's voice, her Carolina lilt softening to a whisper at the end of every sentence, her words spirited away the way her breath was in the end. And Lydia—the strong voice that he could not match, the woman he was not sure he loved. He'd seen her as a delicate creature in need of protecting, with her allergies and her asthma, running the air conditioner year-round, staying inside all the time, on and off the steroids, living on inhalers. He had fallen for her forcefulness, believing it was a defense she threw up against the world, a gesture of defiance—like a Southern belle in front of a burning house. But she was, of course, a Northern girl. And Rudy understood, as he turned to walk to his car, that it wasn't an act, it was real, she was strong, she had never needed his protection and was living with him for some other reason.

A moment later he was kneeling in the leaves, trying to blink his eyes clear between each racking set of sneezes, his hands fumbling, the feed store logo on the burlap swimming all over the place. He sneezed and sneezed, got his fingers into fur and thought too late of claws. He pulled his hand out, a blur of blood before his streaming eyes. It made him think of soldiers, of wounds. He blinked hard and saw blood at his knuckle where his hand gripped the neck of the sack. It unfocused again to a wash of brown and red, and the faces of soldiers from old photographs came to him and the war camp was around him, behind him. He heard noises, the crack of twigs, squirrels in the leaves, but it sounded like men and the wind sounded like sighing. The soldiers had been there, the soldiers had dropped two bullets for him to find. They had slept and ate and smoked around him, they had waited and wondered, lonesome and hungry, and hungry, too, for fighting, without any idea of what it would be like, hungry for it on nothing but faith, it was a wonderful, terrible thing. The boys' faces were so smooth and untested—he wanted to say, take heart, take courage!

He wanted to tell them, I'm here, I'm here. Even though you're gone, and I don't know who you were, no one knows who you were. I am here.

He sneezed into the bag, counted five dark kittens, blurry, swimming, moving, and one, black with tiny white paws, was dead.

He tried and tried to blink his eyes clear. Silently, he said: forgive me, little one, for letting you die. He dragged his sleeve across his nose.

Damn, he thought. Who am I kidding? Heroics.

He dug a small grave with his shovel for the kitten. He knelt in the leaves as he pushed the dirt in the hole with his hands.

He rose. He blinked into the sunlight. "Let's go," he said. "I'll take you other boys to safety."

He wiped his hands on his overalls. The animal shelter would be a twenty-minute drive. He kicked leaves over the grave to cover it, and it looked as if it wasn't even there. So he pushed the leaves back, so that the bare, disturbed dirt would show, not that anyone, except him, would ever see it.

Blood Lake

Jake stomps hard on the brakes and I say, What? What is it?

I am pulling the seatbelt away from my throat. He is gripping the wheel with both hands and staring through the windshield. I look but there's nothing there, just our headlights on the asphalt.

What is it? I say.

But he just keeps staring through the windshield as if there's something out there except there's not.

The scene is all wrong for two reasons. First, we're in the safest and most boring place in the world, our own driveway. It's true that the driveway is steep, and it's tricky making that turn with the Airstream, but it isn't like Jake hasn't done it approximately every Sunday night excepting Januaries and Februaries all our entire married lives. The other thing is that Jake never does that—Jake believes in a soft touch on the brakes, and even when he brakes hard he softens up at the end, a habit he taught me back when we were dating and which always makes me think of him, every single time I have to brake hard in traffic. It doesn't bother me to think of him this way, in fact it's kind of sweet, except sometimes when I resent him for somehow maintaining ownership all these years over this braking technique which I've been doing for so long.

What's wrong, dear? I tend to call him 'dear' when it seems appropriate to be supportive.

He had disrupted my thoughts. I'd been thinking about where we went camping, Blood Lake this place was called. Blood Lake, I had said to him, that's disgusting-sounding. Yes, he said, but we've been to just about every other park in a five-hundred-mile radius. So the only ones left now are the ones with revolting names? I asked. Yes, he said. So this is what I have to look forward to from now on? I said.

Jake doesn't do confrontation. His job is production manager at a watercress farm, but I have no idea what he does there, he doesn't talk about it much. His passion in life is his shiny aluminum Airstream camper. We tow it around to these parks, and I explore the nature trails and the bathrooms and the convenience store while Jake rolls out the awning and sits underneath it with his lawn chair turned around facing in. He sits with a beer in his crotch, staring at the Airstream, its softly rounded corners, the different little fittings and whatnots along its flank. I know this because I've snuck up on him, seen him looking from one thing to another and then quickly to another.

So here we are hanging in the driveway, and I don't understand what's going on, I'm getting irritated, I want to go in the house—*Jake*, I say, what the hell is it?

He slips out of the truck, leaving the door open, which causes the dashboard to begin an obnoxious musical chirping because the key is still in the ignition. I think about sliding over and pulling the keys out, but it's a full-size pickup and all of a sudden it seems too far to me to reach all the way over there. Besides, the overhead light, which is so yellow and bright that I am squinting, will stay on, I know, until the driver's side door gets closed again.

I get out, feel my foot press into the grass—the truck takes up the whole driveway—and I walk around the front of the truck, followed by the faint silly chirping from the key in the ignition. When I reach his door I slam it, loud. The yellow light is snuffed and the noise shuts up. I make my way down the side of the Airstream.

I reach the end and turn the corner, expecting to see Jake. He's not there. Jake? I say. I stand still and listen but he doesn't answer.

Jake? Softly now, as if I know he isn't going to hear me.

I walk out in the street, around the butt end of the Airstream. He's right there, crouched down and humped over like he's sad or crying, which looks odd. That's when I see what he's looking at, and understand all at once what has happened, except that I don't understand because I don't get at first what the object is I'm looking at—all I see immediately is that the Airstream has grazed this peculiar obstacle that has appeared out of nowhere. I stare at it. It has reflectors, the kind they put on bicycles, and these wink at me in a deep red color and I see what it is: a cross, a knee-high wooden cross, a memorial cross to someone dead.

Oh my God, Jake, I say. He does not speak. I don't say anything else, but watch as Jake gently turns it so it is not touching the Airstream. It moves easily, having come a little loose in the collision, soft as that was—I try to remember feeling the impact, but there is nothing there to remember. Jake is the only one who felt it.

He gets back in the truck, starts it and pulls it the rest of the way up, gets out and locks the door. Meanwhile I look at the cross, which stands just very slightly crooked and, because I was born a Catholic, it reminds me of things.

Then we go inside and don't say anything else about it that night, but I lie in bed thinking what it had to mean: what it meant had happened while we were camping.

I dreamed of voices I'd heard that came back to me from the campground, from gas stations, rest stops. Voices you overhear in bathrooms, incomplete sentences. They trail off when you walk away: I told him there was no way . . . Everybody saw it but nobody . . .

I remember I also dreamed of things you see driving at night—something in the road that looks like it's solid but then you see it's just a leaf.

I got up in the morning after Jake had gone to work, and I wandered through the house with my coffee, thinking about the cross outside. Then I got dressed and went out to look.

In the morning light, kind of bright and damp, everything looked different. The Airstream was still there, large as life, but it didn't dominate the scene any more—there were the other houses, which in our neighborhood are all on half-acre lots and all sit kind of alone and high on their lawns. There were birds flying around, a big cloudy sky, and our front yard, covered with dew, sloping down from the house to the road. Down at the bottom, in the shallow ditch at the edge of the street, there it was. From the door I could see the top of it sticking up and the crosspiece, but the bottom of it was hidden from view. I thought, I wish it were lower, so you couldn't see it from here.

I went down. I circled around it, walked out in the street. It was a simple thing, made of hardware store lumber with the edges sanded smooth and maybe colored with a cheap walnut stain. It looked sturdy enough, its pieces perfectly straight and its round reflectors lined up nice and symmetrical. Down in the grass at its foot—the grass is longer there, because the ditch stays pretty moist—half hidden in the grass I noticed what looked like a flower, a rose. I touched it and that's what it was, a plastic red rose, kind of cheap the way it looked and felt.

I scoured the slope of the lawn with my eyes, and I realized I was looking for clues. I had a creepy feeling because all around the cross and sloping up the hill it looked like nice suburban grass, ready to mow in a few more days. Pretty thick, pretty smooth, little bit of weed, dandelion leaves and such. There was one place on the slope above the cross that looked dented, and I wondered if it had been like that before, and then walking along the ditch a little ways I saw a sort of an elevated ridge a couple feet long, running diagonally up the slope. I touched the grass there—the turf appeared cut— I sunk my fingers in the grass and lifted and the whole grassy mat came up in my hand, cut sharp as if a knife had sliced the earth. I laid it back down, and patted it firm, trying to make it look undisturbed, but the slight ridge remained, looking just as I'd first seen it, and I realized someone else must have tried to press it down the same way.

Then it seemed easy, I started seeing things which were maybe there and maybe weren't. A little farther down the ditch, the grass looked smeared just where it met the asphalt of the road. The grass in the ditch near it looked bent, as if it had been flattened but was trying to stand up again.

I stood and stared at the cross. I felt silly and humble at the same time. I wondered if any of the neighbors had seen it, if somebody perhaps was watching me right now. I resisted the urge to scan the windows of the houses along the street. I felt self-conscious, I felt almost embarrassed about this cross on my lawn. But I felt respectful too. I didn't know what to do with my hands, I held them together in front of me, kind of nervously, which made me look like I was praying. Then I went inside and stayed there.

I got on the internet, but couldn't find anything about a wreck in our neighborhood. I thought, who do you call? I called the police and spoke with a woman who seemed very busy or annoyed or both. When I asked her if there had been a car accident around here, she said she had nothing to tell me. Like that—she repeated it, in fact—*I have nothing to tell you*. It seemed like probably just her way of talking but I did wonder what she meant.

I happened to be looking out the window when Jake came home. I watched as he coasted his car to a stop at the bottom of the front yard, just as he did every day, but he sat there for a minute and then backed up about ten feet. The cross, I thought. When he came inside he was frowning, and he told me he'd forgotten about it all day until he saw it when he parked the car.

We spent the next couple hours trying to figure out how to talk about it, in between eating dinner and watching TV. We would circle around it and then circle away again. I mentioned my call to the police, my fruitless internet search.

What do you think happened? I said.

Simple, he said. Some kid flipped his car on our street.

How do you know it was a kid?

'Cause you would only expect kids would put up a cross like that.

I imagined a funeral: stoic-looking Dad and shell-shocked Mom, and lots of puffy-faced, tear-streaked teenagers milling around. The minister intoning, One taken from us so young . . .

You know what's really strange? I said. It's like there's almost no damage to the grass or the street. How can you have a car wreck that bad and have hardly anything to show for it?

I don't know. Whole thing is weird.

What are we going to do?

About what?

About the *cross*.

Nothing. Nothing we can do. Live with it.

What if, what if it's not even in the right spot. Maybe the reason there's nothing to see is 'cause they put the cross next to the wrong driveway—

It's not in the wrong place. There's no possibility of that.

But Jake—

Honey, we've got to leave the damn thing alone.
Our discussion was over. But *I* wanted to get rid of it.

I tried to imagine a carload of kids driving around with a wooden cross in the backseat, the cross lying across their legs, thighs bumping, all knee to knee in the backseat. Nighttime, it's dark out, they're looking out the windows into the dark, watching the lights go by, not saying much because they're thinking about their friend. Their friend has a name like Amber or Michelle or Stacy, or Brad or Craig or Josh.

It's nighttime because it's twenty-four hours since their friend died. They spent the first part of the day calling everybody on the phone, saying Did you hear what happened? and waiting for the answer, either Yes! and then they would start crying again on both ends of the phone, or No, and then there would be a tiny silence, and then the caller would spill the news and the shock and the crying would begin again.

Only the girls would actually cry, I realized. What would the boys do when they called each other? A lot of Wow, man. Wow. Wow, I don't believe it. Lots of empty sad pauses, some choking up but no sobbing. I assumed that mostly the girls were doing the calling, so that when they called a boy, he could be stunned and sad, and she could do the crying for both of them. And he might try to comfort her, and she would feel better, and in a couple weeks maybe the same boy would call her up for a date, but that's too cynical, it's not the way I felt about it, so I changed the subject in my head.

I thought, whose idea was it to do the cross? Maybe the boys came up with that.

So the next part of the day they spend driving to hardware stores for wood and screws and sandpaper, and then to somebody's dad's garage where they run drills and saws. Then more phone calls to get everybody together, and by the time they're all in the car and they know what they're doing it's late and it's dark, just like it was the night before, and maybe they think about this as they ride, the cross vibrating on their knees, looking out at the shadows and lights of the strange neighborhoods they are passing through.

They think they know where they're going. Someone was there this morning. They have heard the spot described. They are reliving the fatal moment in their heads—they pull up to the curb, this is it, someone says, this is the place. They picture the car on its side, the car that is no longer there, the broken glass, the headlight staring blindly into the grass. They get out and the boys start pounding the cross into the ditch and the girls are not crying now. Everyone is hushed and standing around watching with the car doors open and the engine running and it hardly matters under the circumstances that they're two blocks away from where it really happened.

Oh well, I told myself, nice try. Of course, Jake was right, they weren't in the wrong place. That sort of mistake just doesn't happen.

So I too spend the next days looking at the ditch imagining the side of the car crunched into the slope, the blood on the metal, the crooked eyeball of the headlight laying a beam along the peaceful grass.

Jake, I said, why isn't there broken glass out there?

Maybe the windshield didn't break.

I looked at him sideways. No way, I said.

Maybe it was a motorcycle. Maybe it was a pedestrian, hit and run. Maybe they swept up the glass.

I thought of the sound of the sledgehammer pounding the cross into the dirt, and the sound of a broom on the pavement, sweeping.

One night in bed he turned over and started acting the way he does when he wants to make love, but all I could think was no, no, no.

◆ ◆ ◆

So we sort of got used to having it there. We came and went from the house, walked right past it. Jake went out and mowed the lawn. A neighbor stopped to talk to him. Jake killed the lawnmower and they stood there conversing just a few yards from the cross. The strange thing was it didn't even seem so odd to me. I never asked him whether they talked about it.

I felt I had missed my chance, myself, to ask the neighbors if they had seen anything. The woman across the street who was always walking her two dogs, for example. I had waited too long. It would seem strange of me to start asking now. Like what, I had only just now noticed?

Maybe it's not something you talk about with the neighbors—any more than you talk about someone throwing a TV set out on the lawn, or locking their kid out of the house and the subsequent screaming back and forth through the door all night, both of which were things I'd seen living in my neighborhood.

Maybe ignoring the cross was the neighbors' way of reassuring us that everything was normal, that it didn't bother them, so we wouldn't feel uncomfortable. I guess you could say it was a nice neighborly thing.

But when I saw them out there chatting together over the lawnmower it felt to me like a conspiracy.

And I still wanted it gone. I wanted it just to disappear.

Jake tried to get my mind off it. He wanted to watch movies on TV a lot and he even wanted to go *out* to the movies. He would never get popcorn because afterwards he wanted to go out to eat. At the restaurant he would talk about places he wanted to go camping, and when that ran out, he would talk fondly of camping trips from the past.

Remember when we first got the Airstream, he said, and we went to that little place by the river, and there was nobody else there because it was so late in the year. And you thought it was cold and you wouldn't come out of the Airstream till I made a big fire.

And, I thought, that was the night we took a walk away from the fire so we could see the stars, and we made love up against a tree. And we were warm then, but I could see my breath.

His eyes smiled at me. The food here is good, he said, we should come here more often.

I said sure.

In the mornings, Jake started getting up earlier than usual, and bringing me coffee in bed. At first he brought me things to eat too, toast or a donut, but I can't eat that early. It was cute, seeing him lay a plate with a fat donut on it, like an offering, next to my head.

Honey, I said, you don't have to be so nice to me.

Just trying to keep you mellow.

Cut it out, I'm fine.

See, it's working.

Very funny.

I know it's funny! He was laughing.

No, it's not! It's not funny! I said, and he stopped.

Then I felt bad because he was just trying to be nice, but I was mad at him too because he can be such a pain in the butt.

I started going down at night to look at the cross, just before I went to bed. I would take out the trash or go lock my car or take something to the mailbox, and I would stop just a minute by the cross and look at it. It seemed right to look at it in the dark, easier to imagine it. You stupid kid, I'd say. How'd you manage something so stupid? Were you drinking or goofing around or what? Think how your parents feel. But then sometimes I would stop myself—you crazy woman, who are you talking to. There's nobody here. Then I would get angry—why the hell is this dumb cross at the bottom of my yard! Why me? It is the right of every American, I protested, to be free of anonymous crosses erected for unknown dead people.

I went down there one time and I said, Amber or Michelle, or Brad or whatever your name is! Angry because I didn't even know who it was or anything about this person. I kept my voice down, like a hiss. I said, why is this necessary? Why is it necessary for this cross of yours to be planted at the bottom of my lawn? What is the meaning of it?

I kept going out there. Jake never noticed because I kept my visits short.

Where's the broken glass, Michelle? I imagined her with chips of windshield all in her hair. Why am I talking to you, you're not even buried here, you're buried somewhere else. Is it necessary for you to have two memorials? Presumably somewhere you have a real grave, a nice piece of shiny granite. What if this cross disappeared sometime, would you be any less remembered? Any less dead? But the cross had nothing to say. Its round red eyes just shimmered in the little bit of light that was leaking from the house across the street. Like a warning, don't do this here again, don't wreck your car here, it's already been done, don't die here. Warning people away from my little bank of grass, but nothing to warn them away just down the street. Go do it someplace else, don't do it here, once is enough, can't keep it from happening but don't do it here. It was a warning. But the cross could not save a single life.

I went inside, Jake was already in bed. I got in beside him, and made love to him, not enthusiastically, but not insensitively.

Eventually Jake's niceness began wearing thin. I knew it was an expenditure of energy that couldn't last. We stopped going out to movies and paid less attention to what we watched at home. Jake got involved in various diversions and chores and he went out and washed and waxed the

Airstream, which took all weekend. I watched as the little rivulet of soapy water trickled down the driveway and curled into the ditch around the base of the cross.

I got up early one day and sat down across from him at the breakfast table. He had his back to the big bay window that looks out on the front lawn, and the sun coming in made a kind of halo around him. He was making contented chewing noises, his mouth full of cornflakes. I was glowering at him.

What's the matter? he said.

Nothing.

You want to go camping this weekend?

Where?

I don't know. It doesn't matter.

Ha. Remember what happened the last time we went camping.

This conversation ended, followed by silence. He left, and I stood at the window and watched him marching down the driveway, a spring in his step from two cups of coffee— he always was a morning person. Looking at the back of his head, I imagined him humming or even whistling as he went. He neatly sidestepped the cross, making a crisp turn around it to his car.

Fuck you and your bloody Airstream. I stomped my foot on the floor.

It got worse as the day wore on. At first I wanted to cry but I just couldn't, so I gave up on that. I paced the house but I didn't want to go outside. I started to turn the radio on but then I turned it off again.

I made dinner for him when he got home but I didn't eat any. I turned the pages of a magazine while he watched TV. Finally it got late and I went outside to get something from my car.

I started down the driveway, my eyes on my feet—dark blurry blobs moving over the black pavement, touching down without a sound. The air was quiet, suffocating—I could hear a car a few blocks away, but so far off and muffled it didn't sound real. I thought, some loud noise should explode out of that sound.

And then I saw, and then I started yelling.

No, put it back! Put it back!

Jake came out of nowhere, came up behind me and crossed his arms around me to make me stop, and said, Okay, okay.

Put it back!

Okay.

Get your hands off me!

Okay.

No! I said. Wait. Stay here with me.

We stood together, not looking at each other, but it was dark so it was easy to keep our eyes to ourselves. I said, we have to put it back.

He said, okay. I know.

I think he really did know.

He went and got it, and we did it together, I held it straight while he hammered, gently, so the neighbors wouldn't hear us.

We planted it deeper this time, more solid I guess but so it was lower too. We got it all the way in, almost down to its crotch, its hub, its neck, whatever you call that, where the sideways piece goes across. I would have kept going even, but Jake said, no, no, that's enough, that's enough, and he made me come away. I pressed my face to his chest just to feel his breathing in and out push against my cheek.

Dee Told Bea

Dee imagined the sound in her ear was a message, a different one every time. It said *here we go again!* or *time to get perky!* but it did that, through the miracle of technology, in a single electronic syllable that lasted exactly one second (she timed it once).

Sometimes the sound translated to what it did as it escaped her headset and entered her ear: it sounded like *leak*, or *seep*, or *bleed*. She'd be thinking about this while the ghost on the other end was talking (they were all ghosts—she stared at the computer screen but could never see what they looked like, only what they wanted to buy, and she did what she could with this; if a woman was ordering, for instance, a "Seabreeze" acrylic sweater—cowl neck and wide horizontal aquamarine-and-white stripes—Dee used this to construct an idea of her).

Dee was briefly married, long-widowed, and had worked at the call center for years. She tried to tell her sister how they used to say, *somebody* has to stand on all those assembly lines but now it's *somebody* has to answer all those phones. Her sister told her to cut it out, stop it already, and other three-word packages of advice. Her sister's name was

Bea—they were twins, and Dee hated the rhyming name thing but Bea said, let it go.

Bleak, said the phone. "Hello, this is Dee, thank you for calling blah blah blah." And the ghost said "Blah blah blah," and Dee clicked on a picture of a yellow dress that looked like a potato chip with sleeves.

To distract herself, Dee thought about how airplanes at night look like stars at first. How you can imagine things about them, especially if you blur your eyes. Then she thought how blurry everything looks in the rain. How, in a light rain, she could forget, between wipes of the wiper blades, that she had turned them on to intermittent, and then she'd remember when they went across again. This reminded her of the car she and her gentleman friend Tad rented one time, how it had about a dozen speeds of intermittent wiper that took forever to dial through if you wanted to get to non-intermittent and made her wonder who could ever possibly need that many gradations of intermittent wiper.

Bea made fun of Tad's name, said it sounded like a ukulele guy in an old surf movie.

Eeek, said the phone. "Hello," Dee said, "this is Dee, blah blah."

She opened one eye, and clicked on a crude picture of a pair of shoes that looked like a couple of grapes with laces. She did most of her job with her eyes closed, and she always crunched her chair forward against the keyboard, all the way into her not-quite-cubicle so that she almost had privacy. She was a small person, small enough to feel unobtrusive, and her long bangs helped hide her eyes from anyone who might be watching her. She could do the keystrokes without looking, although she did need to peek when she started clicking on icons on the screen—she couldn't find those in the dark.

That, in her opinion, was what the mouse had done for the computer: made it so people's eyes couldn't get any rest. She told this to Bea, who responded, "No one cares. Get a job." Bea often spoke in three-word bites.

Tad and Dee had met there at work, in the break room. One day they shared the microwave to cook up a couple of mugs of hot chocolate but then they had to drink it fast before their break time ran out, and it was too hot and they made silly slurping sounds and giggled and acted as if it was critical to finish the entire contents of their cups, while other people came and went, laughing at them. Tad was older than she was but was goofy as an eight-year-old.

Sweet. "Hello, this is Dee," etc. But he didn't work there anymore, he worked at a hardware store because he said if he was going to sell things he wanted to interact with people face to face. He said he wanted to be the happy old hardware store guy, but he had seemed pretty happy before too, on the phones. Dee asked him, "What am I doing here?" and he had no answer. He thought she meant her job, but in fact it was a larger question. It was no use getting into it with Tad, who was incapable of talking seriously about anything, so the other day she had asked Bea.

"Bea, what am I doing with Tad?"

"Got no idea."

"Is it because he is a pleasant man who is nice to everybody?"

"Don't ask me." Bea was not seeing anyone currently. For a while she had gone out with a mumbly college professor, but he moved to Costa Rica as soon as he retired and she ceased to hear from him. Right now she had her eye on the manager/heir poised to inherit the locally owned grocery store near her house. Bea complained: puny opportunity; smelly, small; terrible selection. It wasn't clear if she was talking about the store or the man. But her kitchen cabinets were full to overflowing—she had canned goods and cereal boxes stacked on the counter and even on the floor.

"Tad's a good man," Dee had told her sister, "but he doesn't *talk* to me."

"What do you want him to say?"

Speak, said the phone. "Hello," etc. The ghost on the other end said she was going to have to put Dee on hold for a minute. Excuse me? thought Dee.

Dee had one other defense on the job, her Nasty Telephone Voice. It never spoke out loud, and it lived at work, she never brought it home with her. Right now it was saying, "You're putting *me* on hold? You're putting *ME* on hold, you rude bitch?" and so on, waiting for the woman's return, whereupon Dee would politely tell her she needed to put *her* on hold, and then she'd get up and go to the bathroom. A prank like that was bad for one's Call Handling Time, something the Supervisors tracked obsessively, poring over print-outs at pseudo-walnut-veneer desks behind glass walls. Dee's Time had been edging up lately and she might soon be summoned to one of those glass rooms for a talking-to, which worried her in a general way.

Bea didn't know about Nasty Voice, and neither did Tad. There were some things neither of them needed to know. She told Tad, I'm a Teleservice Misanthrope, and then she had to explain what she meant. "And that," Dee told Bea, "is the sort of thing Tad doesn't understand. Even though he's smart, and in fact he's sort of a—"

Geek. It seemed the rude I'm-putting-you-on-hold woman had hung up, and had been replaced by someone else. "Hello, blah blah." Dee clicked on a picture of a suitcase. The screen that popped up said GOING PLACES! She hated that thing.

"Sort of a geek," she had explained to Bea. "He plays computer games all night, silly ones that involve cats or bunnies that jump over things. He has a garage full of old lawnmowers that he tinkers with but never finishes fixing.

He has a goldfish called Computer Chip, a name that makes no sense at all for a fish."

"What's the real problem?" Bea had asked, impatience overflowing. Dee told her about a conversation she'd had with Tad in which they danced around the idea of moving in together, maybe, sometime. She was the one who did most of the dancing, not because he was trying to avoid the topic but because he just didn't have much to say, one way or the other. And perhaps because—though she didn't tell her sister this—he felt badly for Dee, for the nervous, uncomfortable, obviously conflicted way she was talking about the idea of living together. "I think the problem, Bea, is that *I* don't really know how I—"

Feel. "Um, Hello, this is Dee, thank you blah blah . . ."

"What?" said the ghost on the phone. "What did you say?"

"Um," said Dee. She went through it again, hello, thank you, etc. Nasty Voice said, "Thank *you*? Surely *you* should be thanking *me* . . ."

"Where am I calling to?" the ghost on the phone asked. Dee got it all of a sudden. She could see the woman sitting on the floor with a stack of catalogs in front of her. She could see them shifting, slipping, their glossy covers skidding over each other, downhill, sideways. It was an oil slick of catalogs around her on the floor, and she had no idea which one she had dialed.

Here's somebody more pathetic than I am, Dee wanted to tell Bea.

"Bea, sister, tell me what to do about Tad? Part of me thinks it isn't worth it, going through this, too much like work."

Bea had replied that men are a pain, better to be independent, self-sufficient. Dee reminded her that until recently her kitchen was as challenged as Old Mother Hubbard's, and now look at it. No place to even set down a spoon.

"Do you want to get married or something?" asked Bea, incredulous.

"No—"

"What do you want?"

"I don't know," said the ghost on the phone.

"I don't know," said Dee.

Dee remembered when she and Tad rented that car, the one with the too-generous intermittent windshield wipers, they were in Atlanta for his ninety-two-year-old uncle's funeral, he wanted her to go with him though she was never sure why, and afterwards they were in some shopping center and they got out of the car and a woman stopped them and rolled down her window and asked if there was a big furniture store around there. Here they were, being accosted in a parking lot in a strange city on the day of a funeral, being asked this ridiculous question. Dee took Tad's hand, feeling bad for him—his eyes were all puffy from crying— and she stepped forward, determined to get rid of the woman, thinking here's something I can do, it's the least I can do, allow me. She said, "Listen here, lady!" or something equally brusque, but Tad pulled her back, gently, and kept hold of her hand and said: "A big furniture store? No, but there are a couple of places near here that sell small furniture, if you'll settle for that." He was grinning. The woman just drove away. He squeezed Dee's hand.

"Well," said Bea, "when you do talk to him, what exactly *does* he say?"

"I told you, he doesn't say."

"He must say something."

"Damn it, Bea, you're not listening." But this sounded a lot like her Nasty Telephone Voice, which was upsetting.

I have to watch my Voice, thought Dee. I have to watch my Time. My customer is contemplating her navel on the other end of the phone.

"It's like this," she had told Bea, "he says he's been

thinking about selling the house, getting a smaller place now that his kids are grown."

This was a few days back, and a week or so after the uncomfortable conversation about moving in together. He had sat at her kitchen table, cutting an onion with a little serrated knife. The onion was big and so were his fingers but the knife was small and he looked like a little kid with his shoulders hunched over the table, and especially with his tongue sticking out the corner of his mouth because he was concentrating. He couldn't chop onion and talk at the same time, so he would stop and look up at her to speak, look up from under his big bushy caterpillar eyebrows, and he pushed his stringy gray hair back with his forearm because his fingers were all oniony, and he smiled at her, still looking like a child, but a grown-up child because his eyes were so twinkly and kind and safe. And none of this could she explain to Bea, how he looked, only tell her his words. He said, "I think I'm ready for a new place."

"Sounds like he may be including you in there somewhere," said Bea.

"I guess." The whiny woman on the phone was gone. She hadn't been able to make up her mind.

Dee remembered his face. She wondered if it was possible to love someone for being inarticulate, not just in spite of it.

Bea sighed. "Sounds like it's up to you."

Dee thought, do I hold out for some other kind of man, at my age?

Deep. But she cut the caller off, by mistake.

Weep, and she cut that one loose too.

"I think I'm ready for a new place, is all he said . . ."

Bea said, "Maybe that's the best you're gonna get."

Dee realized that, of course, Bea had been talking about his *words*—she meant those *words* are the most you're gonna get from him, but Dee worried that *he* was the best she was going to get—

"Maybe it will do?" Bea said.

Again, Dee knew she was talking about his words, she was saying that maybe his words would do. But Dee was wondering if *he* would do. And she knew it sounded awful, even to herself it sounded awful to say such a thing about a person, such an obviously good, warm person. Maybe *he will not do*.

But then Bea was speaking in those impatient, three-word bites of hers. "This is hopeless. Give it up." And in a quiet voice: "Just take him. Just be happy. You need him."

And that's when Dee realized her sister wasn't talking about his words. She had known, all along. They were twins, after all.

But no, thought Dee, she's still not getting it. How can I say it without coming out and saying it? I'll just have to say it, I'll have to say, what if it *won't* do, what if *he* won't do—

"You'll do, Dee."

Me? thought Dee. "What?" she said.

"You heard me. You will do."

Dee remembered that day in the parking lot, how she had behaved toward that woman in the car, how she'd been so mean to her while Tad was so nice. He was so darling and she was such a—

Creep. Her finger floated over to the disconnect button on the phone, and squished down on it.

And when he was sitting at her kitchen table, his hair in his face, his clumsy fingers crowding the knife, how he started to sniffle but this time it was the onion making him cry.

"Dee?" said Bea.

And the way he goofed around with all the intermittent speeds of the windshield wipers, his eyes still all red and puffy. What kind of man can play and cry at the same time like that? This was what she wanted to know.

"What do you think?" said Bea.

Dee thought: He loves me.

"Dee?"

Dee's Voice was quiet. Her Time was up. "He loves you," and it was Bea's voice in Dee's head, though these were never words that Bea had said. In fact, at this point, Dee was none too sure where their remembered conversation left off and her own thoughts, in the now, began.

Dee? The callers were blowing away like petals off dead flowers in the wind. They were falling away, helpless as dominoes. They were gone, like ghosts who turn toward a door and without opening it, walk right through.

Dee?

Dee?

See?

The Mover

Tom didn't want to stare but felt his eyes were being pulled into the peephole in the center of the door. There was nothing else to look at. He had no way of seeing the large brown eyeball blinking up against the other side of it.

The woman inside the house stood on tiptoe with her fingertips spread and pressed to the door, and her eye so close to the tiny window that her lashes brushed it when she blinked. She whispered, "oh, oh, oh." She thought the man looked like a person in a bubble, with blue sky and clouds and parked cars trapped in it with him. She thought how bubbles popped or floated away, but this was not a bubble, this was a man, and he was staring at her through the peephole, and she said "oh" in a louder voice and sprang back and shrank down, and stayed that way.

Tom looked down, studied the concrete step. She was expecting him. She had demanded he come. He wished she would answer the door because he might start to perspire soon.

The woman came out of her crouch, feeling her way up the door with her hands. She blinked rapidly at the peephole. Ah—he was not looking at her. She breathed in and out, fast little puffs of breath.

The door swung wide open and Tom saw a small woman, standing with her feet apart and her toes turned in, one hand on the doorknob, the other hiding her mouth.

"Hi, I'm Tom Abel," he said. He tried a professional smile.

"Right," she said, and stepped back. He moved, broke into huge lumbering forward motion, right through the doorway into her living room.

"China shop!" she said.

"Excuse me?"

"Nothing."

"You've got this place all packed up," he said. There were a dozen boxes spread about the floor, all of them sealed with tape—none of her personal effects lying around exposed.

The first thing he noticed about the way she looked at him was how she did not look at him. Her eyelids were an oily violet color, and she had long lashes. She wasn't pretty but she wasn't ugly; she had an interesting face, high cheekbones and a pointed chin, like the outline of a heart. She had unusual hair—long, brown, and very thick, the kind that is textured but not curly, hair that does not reflect light.

For her part, she had already seen him through the peephole. She knew his shape and height, having translated these from the bubble. But he was so big suddenly, and so sharp in his details, which she hadn't been able to see through the lens: the thigh-parts of his jeans, the way they were stretched to shape, the rest of him stretched to shape too, everything about him broken-in—his worn leather belt, the crinkly look of it. And crinkly little lines around his eyes. She tried not to see any of it. She watched him, sideways—his knees, the side of one thigh. Big burly guys like him made her uneasy. She didn't understand them, their size, the way they felt inside their skin.

She thought, *he is worrying my boxes with his eyes.* She almost spoke, almost said *superman,* because she was thinking of his x-ray eyes, but caught herself when she remembered she had just said *china shop.*

She blinked quickly, looked all around but not at him.

He imagined her boxes weren't packed very tight, and resisted the urge to pick one up and shake it.

She tried to figure out if she should be afraid, all alone in the house with him. He tried to figure out if there was something wrong with her.

Tom had a little rhyme he tried to use now, to remind himself: *salesman's face, glued in place.* Before going into business for himself he had not been a face. He had been a body and the moves it made—shoulders to shoulder cartons and crates, hands to hand off tools to his partner. His thighs had grown hard tensing under load, his chest broad and thick the same way. He never thought about his body, he perceived it only as the vehicle of his action—he didn't think about it, look at it, did not even feel it except at the end of a week with overtime in it. Then he felt his body melting, delicious and sore, into the elixir of that first cold beer on an empty stomach—he had a small stomach that filled quickly with beer.

Tom, for years, had been happy to work for others. He lifted and pulled, he grunted; he cursed pianos but never held a grudge. He got on with it, the best attribute in a mover. What he liked about the work was that there was no one to notice or judge him. He would nod to the lady of the house as he passed by, but his hands were full and he did not have to stop for her.

He laughed, he joked. He scratched his scrotum but he never spit.

Gradually, over a year or two, Tom had begun to notice furniture. He had always accepted the need to protect fabrics and corners, and he was good with the plastic wrap, winding it tightly around and around till the surfaces underneath became cloudy, mysterious. It was this obscuring he noticed first, how a gleaming lacquered table edge could become unrecognizable. He began to linger on this, remembering how the edge had been before he covered it. And he recalled it not so much with a visual image but with touch: imagined—felt—his finger run along the slippery table edge. He looked forward to the unwrapping, to stripping away the layers of cloud to find the piece unchanged, transported. He realized these feelings were strange, and he told no one about them.

He was not discriminating with his affections. He very soon became promiscuous. Understandably, it was Chinese silk and sweet clear rosewood that had first caught his eye, but he was a blue-collar man on the inside as well as out— he had grown up breathing in his mother's cigarette smoke and eating peanut butter out of the jar; his father was a pipe fitter. Consequently he began to take note of the humbler things that people took with them when they moved— wooden chairs with loose rails, table lamps with dirty shades. Much stranger were the funny objects, the inexplicables, the big grinning Buddha, for instance, out of place in the American Colonial living room. Sometimes he felt he was stumbling over secrets, whose full meaning and significance remained hidden: like the larger-than-life framed print of snarling great danes he took down from above a woman's bed, where it had been hanging, not very straight.

But he felt for them all, all the pieces, more and more, with the same feeling, and he wrapped the stained and wobbly kitchen table with as much tenderness as he gave the immaculate solid cherry dining room, though more to bind it against crush and collapse than to protect its skin from wounds.

His life became an assemblage of other people's things, which he collected but did not covet. The collection moved through his dreams at night, where its pieces were distorted and hybridized: a refrigerator grew chair legs, a bed had a headboard of small appliances composed as if all copulating together. Sometimes he saw furniture that moved, in a parade, without the aid of the mover, through some vague house he did not recognize.

Inevitably he began to see himself as a mover, define himself as such, in much the way he supposed a priest might see himself as a priest, or a soldier as a soldier. Tom decided he was drawn to moving because he had an interest in people's furniture, in their objects. He was a tangible guy; he liked people's tangibles.

The men Tom worked with moved on, tended to try other things. He noted their nonchalance about dropping one line of work and picking up another. He realized, in an undramatic moment, that he would be a mover forever, and it was this realization that made him decide, with the deepest reluctance, to start his own business.

He preferred, anytime, the wide open front door and back door of moving day over the hesitant talk, the unknowing, the standing around of scouting missions like the one he was on now. It was what he hated about having his own business, but there was no one else to do this part, and no way he could go back to taking wages from another man who did it for him.

"Thing is," she said, "I didn't know if I was gonna use you or rent a U-Haul, I mean, I still don't know—I mean—" She didn't want to tell him how she didn't have anyone to help her move, a fact she'd only realized lately although she knew she must have known it all along. She guessed she had pushed it out of her mind when they moved the big fence, that is, when she could not find the big fence that was supposed to be there, where she was meant to make a right turn according to the directions they had given her to find the new house. At that point it wasn't her new house, but now it was, or would be.

"When is it," she asked him, to change the subject, "that a house you're moving to becomes *your* new house? Is it when you sign the lease, or not until the day you move in? Or is it when you very first lay eyes on it and know you're going to live there?"

Tom pondered this as a serious, philosophical moving question, which he considered he might be qualified to address, though such a question had never been posed to him before.

She stood remembering driving through the new neighborhood for the first time, thinking I'm going to *move* here, I'm going to move *here*. It felt alien to her, she felt like an intruder, but she told herself that if she paid the rent then the house would be hers, and that she would gradually feel comfortable claiming it, little by little, unpacking her things and moving them around. She would move them around forever if she had to, if that's what it took.

Tom meanwhile searched himself for an answer to her question—when did a new house become one's own?—but realized that although he was a mover by trade, he'd had little experiencing, himself, moving. He discovered he had no strong impression of what it was to stand in his customers' shoes.

"I don't know," he said. "I guess it varies from person to person." This sounded vague and unsatisfactory to him.

"My new house—there's all these big roads you have to take to get to it, you know, almost like freeways—" He thought, what is *almost* like a freeway? "—lots of lanes, you know, and you feel like you have to stay in them, it's like swimming, you know, *laps*, in a pool." But of course you have to stay in them, he thought, what else would you do?

"But then you get off these roads all of a sudden," she said, "and you're on these *little* roads that are as skinny as they can be and still be two-lane roads, and even this changes when you get to be a block or two from the house—the yellow line stops, and the road skinnies down, it's just black with a little white line painted down each side which I think is supposed to keep you out of the ditches—"

She stopped here and looked thoughtful. She was scared of the ditches and she knew it.

He was going to say something, about her furniture—she didn't have any, as far as he could see—when she started up again.

"Lemme tell you about the ditches!" Maybe if she talked about them, it would help. "It's like this. The place I'm moving to, you could sink to your ankles in the water table. The water table is so high, all it's waiting for is a little bit of rain, to just come right up out of the ground. They used to have septic tanks down there, before they put in a sewer line, and they would pump out the tanks but they would just seep full of water again, just ooze full of water before you could even flush a toilet." She saw again the image that had formed in her mind when her landlord-to-be had told her about it: the big tank, in the pitch black underground, perfect blind darkness, slowly sucking full of water. "And when they put in the sewer," she continued, "they left all the tanks where they were, and they're still there, in everybody's yard, big water-filled tanks, sloshing, invisibly, in the dark."

She beamed. He waited.

"And the ditches?" he said.

"The ditches! by the road are just great long puddles. They're four feet wide and four feet deep. They're so big, I swear, if you ran off the road, your wheels would just hang up and spin in the air. They go on and on, like long canals that follow beside the roads—where they have to run under people's driveways they go through lengths of corrugated pipe—you know the kind, that big aluminum or galvanized, whatever it is, with the big ribs."

He nodded.

"There's frogs in the pipes," she said, her eyes getting big, glancing all around the room. "They live there. Huge green shiny frogs that stick their heads out of the water, at the mouths of the pipes."

He pictured the slick green skin of the frog, saw the tangle of boggy plants sliming just under the water's surface, imagined the black water spinning with mosquito larvae.

"There's mosquitoes hatching in there," she said.

"Yeah," he said. He knew.

"They swim around, in all directions, little tiny pale worms, they roll up toward the surface, and roll down again. The water's dark underneath and they disappear down, and you can't see the bottom."

Don't the frogs eat them? he wondered.

"The grass is squishy," she said.

The grass?

"There's no sidewalks, and the roads are so narrow, if a car comes along you have to step on the little bit of grass between the road and the ditch."

He understood, saw her now: walking down the lane, peering in the ditch, forced off the road by a passing car, standing with her feet slowly sinking in the grass. He looked down at her shoes. She wore cheap sneakers, with holes fraying through at the little toes—her feet would get all wet.

"I tried so hard to get a waterfront house," she said, "but the best I could do was get a water-view house and everybody knows that a water-view house is just a house across the street."

Tom had no opinion to offer about this.

"I don't think I want wind chimes. They're okay for an inland house. All I want is the plain sound of the wind, and the water, and the birds. I don't think there's too many birds there. What do you think?"

"I don't know." He felt irritated—he could visualize the ditches now, the frogs and the stagnant water, but he did not know anything about the house she was moving into. "What is your new house like?"

"Oh, it's okay. It's small, it's..." It's new, she was thinking, new to me anyway; it's water-view but I'm not sure I can really see the water—squint between two other houses—oh, how would she feel about it once she was there? No way of knowing.

She thought about what it would be like, moving, how she wouldn't know where anything was, not the big stuff, which would be easy to find, but all the little stuff. It was already that way. Boxes that had seemed unique, special in the way they were put together and distinctive in their outer appearance, no two quite the same, well, they were all starting to look alike. And no way to check on their contents without undoing the tape, but what would be the point in that? No, she must leave them alone, wait to unpack them again and put everything away in all new places. She wondered if this was what bothered her, the fact that she would have to find new places for everything, or the fact that she would never again see her things in their old places which had grown so familiar. No, it wasn't any of this, it was the strangeness of the boxes on her floor, the intrusion of them into an empty space that used to be full. What bothered her was that her whole life had become unrecognizable.

She bit her lip, pulled at it with her teeth, tasted blood. She forgot herself, forgot the mover standing there.

He was saying something about living alone, saying he lived alone too, like she did, something about the advantages, about how it suited him. Poor guy, she thought, he's trying to make conversation because I'm just standing here doing nothing. He seemed sad to her—his humped shoulders, his large clumsy hands clasped in front of his crotch.

She did make him nervous. She would start out talking about something but then just drift away and he'd get the funniest feeling, like he wasn't even there except that he was there. Then he would get self-conscious and wonder what was the polite or normal thing to do. He had brought up the subject of living alone because it seemed a neutral topic that they had in common, not that it came to him that consciously, he just thought of it and started talking about it, though even as he did he wondered what he really had to say on the subject. It occurred to him that perhaps living alone was not the same thing for her that it was for him. He glanced around again at the carefully sealed boxes, as if these held the secrets to this mystery. His own home contained a spare assortment of functional objects which in themselves meant little to him. When he spent time at home, which was rare, he felt contented, looking around, because everything he saw had been earned by his labor—his surroundings were the symbol of his work. And they were just like his work: clean, unpretentious. He liked what his apartment was called, it was true to its name, it was an efficiency.

But he looked at her boxes and wondered. He guessed at their contents, based on what he'd seen in other people's houses. He thought of statuettes and ornate frames around photographs (couldn't imagine, though, the photos within the frames), old baskets, tin canisters made to look antique, and flower vases, teapots, feather boas—actually, he didn't have a clue. It disturbed him, not to know her objects.

She reflected on this living alone business, and decided that it had taught her really only a few things. That a single tube of toothpaste could last an extraordinarily long time. Jesus will be back, she thought, before my toothpaste runs out.

"Living on my own has taught me a couple things," she said. "Like how quickly grass grows when your lawnmower's broken. And how much new lawnmowers cost. And how little interest I have, if I'm perfectly honest about it, in the internal workings of lawnmower engines."

"Yeah, lawnmowers." He didn't have to mow any grass where he lived.

"So I ended up I bought one of those reel mowers, you know, the kind you just push? My neighbor comes up to me while I'm mowing and says 'You can borrow a lawnmower from me if you want.' And I say, 'Excuse me, but this *is* a lawnmower.'"

"I guess you have to keep your sense of humor about these things."

She remembered though—how she didn't crack a smile, how she gripped the bar of the mower more tightly and waited for her neighbor to say something else.

There was a pause.

"Why are you moving?" he asked. It was a new question, a new curiosity for him.

"To get closer," she said.

"Closer?"

"Closer to my one job, but a little farther from my other job."

"What do you do?"

"Here, you tell me what you think—right now I'm driving fourteen miles to my one job three times a week, and six miles to my other job two times a week. My new house will be nine miles from the first job and sixteen miles from the other one, but that one's only twice a week remember. Am I doing the right thing?"

"Um. The first job is—how many miles now?"

"It's fifty-two versus fifty-nine miles total, one way that is. It's more miles after I move. That's the problem, but it cuts the trip I make *three* times a week down from fourteen to nine miles, which is good. Of course the other one goes from six to sixteen but it's only twice a week, and since I'm used to driving fourteen miles, what's the difference between fourteen and sixteen, right?"

"Right." But he was lost, and didn't really care about the mileage problem. He wondered, what kind of car did she drive? Was there anything hanging from the rear-view mirror? "What kind of mileage does your car get?" he asked.

"Oh, my car. Cars intimidate me. Computers intimidate me."

"Me too," he said, but he knew it was different for him, that they weren't talking about the same thing.

"I'm hoping there are lots of birds down there, but I don't know if there are. I'd like to live someplace where there are a lot of birds. I wonder what it's like to be a bird, you know?"

"Yeah."

"I mean, have you ever thought about—how it would feel to have a wing attached, behind your neck, your shoulder." She was thinking of some memory, from somewhere, of a gull perched on a piling, slowly unfolding his wing and then folding, settling it again, like a yawn, like a stretch, in the golden, sleepy sun. "Must be such a curious feeling," she said. "Imagine, creaking your wing open. Reaching."

"Flapping."

She frowned. No, she thought, not flapping. She looked at him.

"The phenomenon of wings," she added quietly, looking off to the ceiling as if training her gaze on some bird that was flying away.

"Yeah," he said.

"One time when I moved," she said, "I was able to move my whole self for like sixty-two dollars."

"How did you manage that?"

"I rented a U-Haul."

Ah, the U-Haul again, he thought. "You don't have much stuff," he said. "Maybe you ought to do that again. If there's just these boxes... and your lawnmower..."

She had a lawnmower story, though she wasn't going to tell it: about the day she was out mowing the grass and the yucca plant stabbed her in the leg, in her one and only varicose vein, and the blood streamed down her leg into her shoe. That's what was wrong with living alone, she thought. No one to tell that story to, no one to show her little bruise to. Stabbed in the varicosity, by a yucca. No one to giggle with. No one to notice that bruise slowly change colors, slowly go away.

"Life is disappointing," she said. "People are disappointing."

The mover didn't understand about that.

She was moving, she reminded herself, moving to a water-view home where everything would be different.

"Wherever you live, that's where you come from, right?" she asked.

The mover didn't know about that. He knew about the brocade on her pillows, if she had brocaded pillows, and the piping around them. The little diagonal seam where the piping met itself. It was just an imaginary pillow; he didn't know what she owned.

But then he thought: what was hidden in her home was missing from his. There was nothing there that would ever help anyone dig out the details of his life.

She grabbed her wiry hair in her hands. "I try to tell myself, don't be sad, don't be sad, but sometimes it doesn't work. What am I supposed to do then?"

He drew a breath and tried to think, but she didn't wait for an answer.

"I think to myself, oh, that sip of coffee tastes good, or that sweet bite of lemon cake that my mother makes. Or the solid feel of a frying pan in your hand, or the softness of a bath towel."

Yes, he thought, all those *things*.

"You're right," he said. "It can be hard. Sometimes, I mean."

She held his gaze for a full five seconds.

"Okay," she said. "We have a deal. Move me."

"Sure, if—"

"Move me, move me."

"Sure—"

"I do have a couple of pieces of furniture in the other room you should see."

Furniture.

He followed her into the next room, thinking, now he would see her furniture, thinking about, imagining the move, the afternoon of the move. He watched the shape of her thick brown hair bob ahead of him, through the doorway. And he yearned and desired, hungered to watch her unpack.

What Do You Remember?

She wriggled, squirmed, just a little, but a little was too much. It started as a shimmy at her hips and twisted up through her shoulders, reminding her of the rippling way a wet dog shakes itself dry. Her eyes were closed but she could see herself all the same: her feet in white cotton socks, her solid, good-looking legs, and the dark blue dress stretched lewdly tight across her hips.

She opened her eyes. What she saw in the dressing room mirror confirmed her expectations except for one thing, the slack, drawn look on her face, jarring because it did not match the view of her face that she carried around inside her, which was freckly and kindly and had always been that way.

The next thing she knew she was reaching for the zipper, the too-tight dress pulling upward in a way that was quite appalling in the mirror, and she yanked on the zipper and it went up though she quit a few inches from the top. Why did I even do that? she wondered.

It looked like a shrunken, perverse Sunday school outfit, complete with sailor-suit trim around the collar. On the hanger it had been a conservative, navy blue linen dress, but every woman knows: the dress when it's on the hanger is not the dress when you put it on. The tag scratched her; she scraped it free of her neck and looked at it—the price was obscenely high. Something obscene about how her hips looked, too, in that dress, and she thought how her hips, at that moment, looked the way her cousin Roberta's hips used to look, but this was a silly, strange idea so she thought of the price of the dress again, and then the oddest memory came to her, of the rehearsal dinner for her wedding twenty years before and something Roberta had said there: he must have more money than you think, because why else would you marry a man twenty-five years older than you?

She hadn't thought of her unkind cousin Roberta in years—unkind, always, perhaps because she had an ugly name and resented this—this is what she had thought when she was a child and Roberta was a child too, a very unkind child.

No, Roberta, you were wrong—but had she said this at the time? She couldn't remember. The rehearsal dinner had been held at a restaurant overlooking the ocean in Maine, in a big dark stone house on an old estate. She remembered the dinner better than the wedding, not the food, but the setting (just as she remembered the site for the wedding better than the wedding itself, which was, in memory, just a blur of bodies in tuxedos and bright dresses, like a photograph taken of the scene, where the people were out of focus because they were moving, while the clean white hotel and the too-pretty village of Boothbay Harbor were frozen sharp and colorful).

She wondered what it was about the big stone house on the cliff that moved her so much more than the picture-postcard charm of Boothbay Harbor. She thought of the stone of the inn as the same stone rising out of the ocean beneath it, that dark rock with the waves crashing on it, looking so wet and black as each wave receded, but she wasn't sure at all it was the same stone, and she couldn't actually visualize the building, though she could sense it around her and feel the power of the waves crashing below and the mystery of the gray sea extending mistily forever. Her parents had given her this, this wildness, this roughness, the evening before her wedding, then spirited her to the protected waters of Boothbay Harbor, to that page from a picture calendar of the quaint hamlets of Maine, to be married.

Even though she was twenty-five years old at the time, her parents had insisted on paying for everything, keeping her childlike in those final moments before her marriage began to the fifty-year-old man she'd chosen.

And now she was forty-eight, and he seventy-three, and they had two kids in college, and here she was all alone in this white, high-ceilinged dressing room, down a long corridor of dressing rooms in a city department store once fashionable but now in a long decline. It was too brightly fluorescent-lit, with pins and lint across its bare tile floor and a door that banged like the door of a toilet stall.

She knew people had assumed she was marrying a father-figure. She reminded herself that she had never thought of him that way.

She thought, I did think of him as handsome and older. Who's to say what was working in the deeper layers of my psyche and so what who cares?

She started to reach to unzip the dress, but hesitated. She'd always figured they were simply jealous—jealous of her handsome groom, jealous, even, of the chance to marry someone taboo in that way—and she shared a coy smile with herself in the mirror.

Then her face was back to business: and I always put it down to a quirk of fate, she told herself, that the man I was destined to marry was older than I was. Destined, as in absolutely destined, as in the first time she saw him she said to herself *here is the man I will marry*, though he was her fiancé's uncle. She had known even as she thought it (*here is the man I will marry*) that the situation would cause a lot of fuss, though she had been as surprised as anybody when the ex-fiancé cut his uncle's bicycle in half with a hacksaw. It couldn't be helped, theirs was a fairy tale love, and in her girlish way she'd assumed that everyone would have to see this. Their love had seemed grand but it had also seemed simple, the love of a girl and a boy, though he was much more a man than a boy, and she was more a young girl than she could know at twenty-five.

The drama of the ex-fiancé and the sawed-apart bicycle had passed from personal memory into family mythology—her boys had heard the story, and that's what it was to them, a story, an old one from another time, an unremarkable part of who they were, and she decided now that something had been lost in translation. She used to think, when they were little, how wonderful it was that they were the accident of their parents' accidental love. She wondered whether they ever thought about that, now that they were so grown. She imagined not. They might think of it, if they ever had children of their own. She couldn't picture herself as a grandmother—she felt much younger on the inside than that. And their father ... That was another thing they took for granted—the age difference between their parents, it was as if it were something that simply was, that had always been, and there had never existed the possibility that things could have gone differently.

The ex-fiancé did not come to the wedding. It hadn't bothered her at the time, but it seemed a little sad now. All that craziness was in the past—he had married, had kids of his own. She was always relieved to think of this.

She tried to remember her husband's face, how he had looked on their wedding day, and she couldn't, it was a blank—she could see his tux, the crispness of it, the way he held himself—he'd always had a way of looking completely relaxed standing completely straight—and she could see his beautiful hands, although maybe this was because his hands were one part of him that had not changed. They were perhaps less firm, a little less there between the skin and the bone.

She had a better picture of herself at their wedding, but that's what it was, a picture, because that long-ago day had become a photograph. In it, she was running down the hotel steps, her magical one-day-only dress lifting like a snowy butterfly's wings behind her, and she was floating on the arm of her new husband, whose face was turned to her in laughter, while she faced the camera, eyes dark and wild, her mouth open, excited, wondering.

The photographer's work had made it last forever even as it turned it into a confection, with the same sugar-white, impossible, inedible look about it that wedding cakes have. It sat on her dressing table, behind other pictures from the years since. She wondered, what did her husband remember of her? Was it, for him, the way it was for her—a grasping for memory, but coming up, only, with the things that hadn't changed—for her, the tall and easy way he held himself, and his beautiful hands.

If she forced herself, she could picture the way he was now, as clearly as any objective observer. But it required effort—the reality did not match the idea of him she carried around inside her, just as her own face, caught by surprise in the mirror, had not matched. She thought, isn't that strange? And she wondered if it was that way for other people, for other women when they looked at their husbands.

This was the exact opposite of how it had been with her children, who instead of persisting in outdated images were in the business of constantly replacing old ideas of themselves with new ones, so effectively that she could never remember quite how they had been before. She had realized this just a couple of years ago, when her elder son's then-girlfriend asked her what he'd been like as a baby. She had resented the question at the time, partly because she suspected the girl was not so much interested as trying to impress, and partly because she couldn't really say. And also because she never really liked that girl. She offered that as a boy he was always outside, always so busy with his friends, never wanted to come in except for dinner, but this obviously did not satisfy the girlfriend who leaned forward waiting for more. How could she explain that as he grew, each phase obliterated the one before it?

This, she suspected, was why parents kept all those framed pictures of their children at different ages—to remind them, to help them keep from losing those certainties completely.

But wasn't it strange that a grown mother like herself, with two grown kids, would be standing here in this overpriced ugly dress that didn't fit, thinking about her wedding? Thinking about things like her cousin's fat hips from twenty years ago, and the way the sea crashed on the rocks at her rehearsal dinner?

She stared at herself, steady in the mirror—the fact is he is still healthy, he is still handsome, he is still in damn good shape, and the fact is he is getting old the way everybody knew he would, he is at last getting old, and I don't know how these two things can be true at once and yet they are.

She reached for the zipper, to get out of that dress and get out of that place, and she took a breath in, anticipating the relief of it as her fingertips grasped the little tongue of metal, and then she tugged on it, gently, but the zipper was stuck.

She paused, just a second, and tugged down again, harder, and it was still stuck.

And then, without a thought, she did the logical thing: she pulled upward on the zipper just a bit, to see if this would free it. It slid upward with liquid ease; she was careful to take it up only an inch. She relaxed her fingers, preparing to reverse direction, and in that moment before she tried again she felt a small, apprehensive tingle. She tugged. It stayed stuck.

She dropped her arms to her sides. She breathed more quickly. A flurry of thoughts ran through her head, confusing, too fast to figure: how if her husband were there he would fix it, how absurd this was since he would never be there, in a women's dressing room, how when he was gone someday, she would have to fix stuck zippers herself, how the world was full of widows with the same problem, how, when you reach a certain age, being a widow is the norm.

Something came back she hadn't realized she had forgotten, a small, terrible episode—their trip to the home improvement store the weekend before. It was an enormous store with endless aisles where it was impossible to find anything, and as they had stood waiting to talk to an employee who was busy talking to someone else, she'd wondered where had all the regular-sized, ordinary hardware stores gone? But looking at her husband, she saw that he was feeling good there, happy in hardware-land; he had an I-can-wait-all-day look on his face as he gazed down the long aisle of light bulbs and electrical outlets and switches and wire. She turned her attention to the salesperson, to his bright orange apron, his bright young face, his head-full of dark chaotic hair—that was the fashion now, hair that was short but looked as if it had tumbled straight from bed—and she noted the genial way he talked to the man he was helping, the way he called him "buddy" and, a moment later, "bud," a big wide open grin on his face the whole time. Done at last, the sales clerk turned to her husband (not to her, she noticed; she was just tagging along, standing by, not a participant but a *wife*). The young man's body transformed—it came over him, she thought, like some lightning-quick costume change in a play—he lost his brash, straight posture and his big grin, and his face fell serious, all patience, a bit dubious, and he made his voice too loud and nodded a lot and bent forward as if speaking to a child. Her husband just kept talking, gesturing with his hands, asking, agreeing, qualifying. And she was glad then to be standing by, to be allowed to be invisible, because she could not bear to be more a part of what she saw.

Tears were starting to her eyes—she had to concentrate on the zipper. She grasped it, prepared to ease it up a quarter of an inch—she would have to move it just a little at a time. It started to slide; it went up, slippery, easy, more and more, all in one slick movement, all the way to the top where it locked, settled, stopped cold.

Oh dear, she thought. Oh no.

It had happened so suddenly. Too fast for her to stop herself.

She pulled at the zipper, down and up and sideways, every angle she could, pulling so hard that her fingers slid off it again and again and stung where the bump on the little metal blade dug into her fingertip. In the mirror her hips spread in battle-stance over her stocking feet planted wide on the floor. No! she thought, please! Her face hardened as she watched her own struggle reflected back to her. No! she thought, no!

She caught her eye in the mirror and her face was fierce and exhausted and ugly. She stopped, blinked at her reflection. She did not try to make her face look nice. All of a sudden she needed to sit down, but there was nothing around her but four bare walls and if she sat on the floor she would split that dress. She wanted out of there, but she couldn't go out, not dressed like that, but how could she stay? Her eyes, in the mirror, gave her back her only option, and it was horrifying—to walk out, in that dress, look for a sales girl, look and hunt and wander around, in front of all those other women milling about the store, watching her while they pretended to be interested in pawing at blouses on racks.

Look at me, she thought. I look just awful. She stared at herself, but was addressing her husband: you used to tease me how marriage to me would keep you young, and I used to tease you back, how maybe it would make me old instead. And now look. Look at me.

She reached again for the zipper, because there was nothing else to do, and it was still stuck, which did not surprise her. She indulged an image of her husband's hands—his beautiful, strong hands at her neck, grasping the errant zipper, working it free. She could see the gentle way they moved, see the thin skin, the blue veins, the bony knuckles she could picture kissing.

Oh, sweetheart, she thought, look at us, look at the two of us.

Her eyes stung again but she stopped herself, stopped any tears before they came. She thought, I must do it, I must ask him, what does he remember of me from long, long ago? Only the unchanging things? Yes, I'll ask him, what do you remember?

She would tell him what she remembered. She would tell him how it was, how if she closed her eyes—like this— she could be back at the inn above the sea, the horizon lost in mist as she stared into it, into her future. The waves rolled in on the black rocks, crashing there into white froth and into spray that drifted upward, reaching her lips with its salt.

The Accidental Inventor

Ahead he could see the road went a little downhill to a cul-de-sac where the trees had been allowed to stay, so he kept going, bumping through the gravelly dips and potholes, eyes straight ahead, careful not to look at the people who were looking at him.

The woman at the office had told him to "go on and take where you want, I'll be able to find you." She smacked gum and made unwavering, uncomfortable eye contact while she talked. She was plump and wore a Steelers sweatshirt that was not new but was so white he could tell she was proud of her laundering skills. That shirt, and the Midwestern flatness of her vowels, reminded him he had crossed a line somewhere, the Philadelphia/Pittsburgh divide, he called it. He felt as if he were still back there, on the crest of one of those long Allegheny ridges, where he'd walked on a trail deep in leaves and held his fingers out as far east and west as he could stretch them, wondering which direction had the most pull.

He'd had to leave the state park down the road when he reached its fourteen-day limit. This was why he was here now, proceeding at a crawl past awnings strung with patio lights, beneath which retired couples in folding lawn chairs lifted their eyes from their televisions to watch him go by. There were older motor homes, a couple of shiny new ones, but old or new, they all looked like they'd been there a long time and weren't leaving anytime soon. They had chrysanthemums in pots, and gas grills, and indoor-outdoor carpet rolled out in the dirt, and they had signs with misplaced apostrophes—"Welcome! The Miller's." They had pumpkins for Halloween. He saw all this, without looking—it bled into his vision, though he was trying not to see. He passed twenty sites on either side of him, close together and all on level concrete pads under the open sun.

As he came downhill a bit, past the bathroom building, the trees filled in—spindly, second-growth hardwoods—and he saw one occupied campsite, with a room-size tent and a cooler and some boxes stacked on the picnic table. It looked transient. The tent was old: yellowing beige canvas with tell-tale gray at the seams and corners, the evidence of mildew past or present, and it hung in a tired way from its complicated frame of aluminum poles.

He could have camped at any site he wanted—the end of the road down there was empty—and ordinarily he would have chosen the spot with the most privacy, but the hard gaze of a little potbellied man in the doorway of one of the travel trailers came back to him, and he pulled into the site next to the one with the tent. He cut his engine, set the brake, and a tall woman stepped out from behind the tent, looked at him, and disappeared again.

She had been wearing a tee shirt—it was a warm day for October—and had breasts of moderate size and no bra. He hadn't meant to look, but it caught him by surprise. He had seen her face, too; she had looked drawn, hollow, not happy. He thought her face looked older than she must be, though he had no exact sense of her age.

He got out of his car. He turned his back on the tent, and stared into the woods of his early retirement.

He got settled in his collapsible reclining chair—silky forest green nylon on a lightweight polymer frame, ergonomically correct headrest, arms with convenient built-in cup holders—ready to relax after his drive. He had just started into a two-day-old *New York Times* and a mug of fresh-ground organic Guatemala Antigua, when a station wagon pulled up next door and children started tumbling out and doors were slamming and a woman was calling *Melanie* in a loud, impatient way.

He turned the page of his paper, to continue reading a story about fashion trends in Japan—a preference for anything pink, it appeared, was the case with the young teen set, and he wondered at what age they grew out of that.

"Oh, the dishes, you brought them," a woman's voice said.

"I told you I would."

He looked over—there were just half a dozen slender trees separating the campsites, and all the leaves were down now. He saw two women pulling plates out of a box, looking at them.

"These will be great," said one of them, the one he'd seen earlier; she had put on a bra. Both women looked up then and saw him looking. His fingers tightened on his newspaper. The plates hung in the women's hands.

He got up, left the paper, moved to the trunk of his car, ducked his head in, and started moving things around. The women's faces, staring at him, stayed with him—the tired-looking one he'd seen earlier, and the other one, maybe her sister because she looked like her but not as thin. They were both tall, with dirty-blond shoulder-length hair, and the same cold eyes.

He rummaged in the trunk. There had to be something he needed there. The propane heater, why not? He pulled this out, and a small gas canister to go with it, and carried it over to his tent, where he made an elaborate show of setting the heater's legs on the ground, moving it around to settle it and get it the right distance from the tent—not too close—and then he had to snake the vent tubing through the flap in the side of the tent that he'd had sewn in specially for this purpose. It was a small tent—a two-person dome with a vestibule, designed for backpacking in high-wind conditions—and he knew from previous nights that the heater would run him out of there unless it was really cold.

He heard car doors closing again. There was talking he couldn't hear, and the high-pitched voices of children and the sounds of their feet running in the leaves. He looked up from where he was kneeling beside his tent, just for an instant, and saw the kids chasing each other—there were two of them, a boy and a girl, maybe four or five or six years old—he wasn't good at judging children's ages. He heard one of the women call out, "See you next week," and then the car started and pulled away. He concentrated on getting the tubing settled so it wasn't twisted. It was suddenly quiet, and he realized, then, that his neighbor did not have a car. Was camping, with two kids, but did not have a car.

Late that night, he got ready for bed—turned on the heater, extinguished his lantern. He got into his sleeping bag and lay on his back, staring up at the dark blur that was the roof of the tent. The night had clouded over, and the darkness was like a cave. He blinked, waiting for his eyes to adjust. He couldn't tell how near or how far the tent fabric was—he reached out his hand, and his fingertips did not touch.

He didn't sleep, but drifted. He wondered what his neighbor's story was. No father in evidence, although maybe he would be along shortly with the car? This would explain the absence of car. Or was she a single mother? Traveling with two small children—perhaps doing a big trip before the children reached school age. Doing the big trip she'd wanted to do as a family before the father (whatever happened there) had disappeared from the story. She was determined to be a family anyway, and to carry out her grand plan—how adventurous and tough! Yet she looked so grim. Maybe the demands of being adventurous and tough were wearing her down. He hoped it wouldn't happen to him.

"What are you going to do out there, in your camping retirement?" It was the voice of his colleague, Adams, and the voices of all the others gathered around him, seeing him off. That's what they called it, his camping retirement, because he had called it that at first, explaining it to them, but when they said it, it didn't sound the same.

"No place to stay?" they asked. He felt the crowd of them, a crowd around him and Adams. "You're just going to camp all by yourself?" They were jealous, not of what he was doing, but of the money. They were all polymer chemists, like him, and they were just as smart, some of them smarter than he was. He could see it in their eyes, the swimming pools and second homes and fancy cars they would buy.

The propane heater was a muffled roar outside the tent. It was getting too warm, just as he'd known it would.

He got up, and slipped out, to turn off the heater. The cold air was a shock. He moved forward, in a crouch, in his tee shirt and undershorts, starting to shiver as he fumbled with the heater. The trees around him were dull, tall shapes; he heard the cracking of twigs—raccoons. He turned back to the tent, and the movement of a lit cigarette, through the thin trees, stopped him—he understood it, how it moved from the smoker's mouth to rest on her knee, even though he could not see her, only this sign of her. His neighbor. Could she see him? No, of course not, and he squatted in the dark beside his tent and watched the red cigarette tip move—drift up, stop at her mouth, flare brighter, drift away again, not to her knee but perhaps to the top of the picnic table—he imagined her, leaning back, exhaling the smoke in a luxuriant way, not looking tired anymore but restful, wearing her tee shirt with her breasts bare underneath, although of course, it was cold, and she must be wearing a coat, and was huddling to keep warm, and looked tired, and hard. He slipped into his tent, zipping up behind him as quietly as he could.

In the morning he had fruit and coffee in his chair and stared into the trees, noting a few, last, tiny brittle leaves hanging on the twig-ends of certain branches, like feathers caught on barbwire. The woman next door was fussing at her children over cereal and juice. He found it terribly awkward and resolved he must speak to her today, introduce himself. Perhaps she could recommend hiking trails in the area?

He looked over her way every minute or two. She got up, carried the breakfast dishes to the spigot; he carefully did not look until she was squatted in the dirt with the water running and splashing. She was wearing a grubby, puffy, gray down jacket, and she kept pushing her hair off her face with one down-puffy forearm. Something about her preoccupation with motherly, household duties made it possible for him to speak. "Hello!" he called out.

"Hi," she said, looking up, her expression too quick to catch as she looked down again—the water was spraying around her knees and feet.

"I'm Carlton Deming," he said.

"Hi," she said again. She stood up, balancing the wet bowls and cups in a precarious stack. "I'm Melanie Dabney."

He cleared his throat. "That's a nice big tent you have."

"It's all right."

"I'm on a cross-country trip." He folded his arms in front of him. "Seeing the whole country."

She looked at him, at his campsite. "In that little tiny tent?"

He started to say *It's not that small* but checked himself. "It's big enough, you know, for just me." The people at work had said, why don't you get a van, or some kind of camper? He had explained to them he wanted to sleep on the ground, and that the state of the art of camping equipment had come so far that there were remarkable products out there. He was a purist, he had told them. "I'm a purist," he said, watching the woman shift the dishes so that they would not touch her dirty coat.

"Oh," she said.

They had laughed at him when he said it—Adams, shaking his head, Mary Gunther exchanging looks with somebody, he didn't know who but he could still see that satisfied shine in her eye.

The woman was standing there, waiting for him to explain—why was he always having to explain things to people? It seemed he couldn't start a conversation anymore without ending up explaining something. He couldn't figure out why people didn't understand the simple things he said.

"Now you," he said. "With that big tent, and your two lively kids"—was it appropriate, he wondered, to refer to them as "lively"?—"now you can do some real traveling with that." There! he thought, flashing her his biggest grin— that was the right sort of complimentary, affirming thing to say. He looked over at her tent, with what he hoped was an admiring, generous look.

Melanie turned away. "Excuse me, sir," she said. "I have to put these things away."

He looked at the trees, looked at his car. Why did she have to call him *sir*? He glanced back at her tent—what a horrid thing it was! But you saw all sorts of things on the road, he reminded himself—yes, he must expect to see all sorts of things, and try not to be surprised.

"It was an accident, really," he said. "There were several of us working on these couple of polymer formulas, and I came up with this stuff that wasn't anything we could use, but it ended up getting picked up and marketed to children in Japan." He didn't feel he needed to tell her it was Adams who put him in touch with the marketing people. "It's called the Foogle. It keeps different foods from touching on your plate."

"It's a—plate divider?"

"It's a flexible, seductively textured, snake-like thing."

"Oh."

"So now I'm retired! And I'm running around the country trying to spend this money before the craze wears off in Japan." He laughed. "Because it will, of course. It's just a fad, after all. I know this. I'm the first to admit it's a ridiculous invention. They wanted me to go to Japan but I refused. I knew what it would be like."

They were sitting at her picnic table. She had been washing dishes at her spigot and he had come over, then followed her when she moved to the table, at first just standing there with one foot up on the bench while she wiped the dishes dry, then leaning against the table's edge, and finally sitting down. All very natural, he thought, very pleasant—surprisingly pleasant.

"In Japan," he said, "I would have been reduced to doing a never-ending infomercial. I would have been a product, just like my invention. And it's a small step from product to caricature, I know how popular culture works, not that I follow it much, quite the contrary." She looked at him— blank but sort of disapproving—maybe she disliked popular culture too. "I told them, no thanks. I would take the money, thank you very much, and light out for the territory."

"Do you have people to stay with, along the way?" It was the same thing his coworkers had asked. There was something derisive in the way they'd said it.

"I'll be camping, mostly. In some pretty remote areas."

"What an adventure," she said. "You'll meet lots of people on the way." This was something else they had said—said it as if they meant to reassure him, though he knew that wasn't what they meant at all.

He wasn't going to tell them he was going to meet people or that he wasn't. In fact he did want to meet people, of course he did, he knew if he was going to discover America, so to speak, he needed to make real human contact out there, it wasn't enough just to connect with landscapes, there was something else he needed to connect with, and he hoped to find it, whatever it was exactly. He was going to connect, he was going to communicate—he might even write a book about it afterwards, which would be a great way to communicate.

When she said it—that he would meet people on his way—was she being sincere, or was she like them? He watched her as she settled the last of her items, a saucepan and its lid, into a big cardboard box. Her hands were bony and red—not feminine-looking. She looked up at him, and smiled; he noticed, though, when she smiled, her face still had that hardness. Her hair hanging around her face did not soften it. He looked away.

"Do you have any family?" she asked.

"Not really. None to speak of."

"Well, I'm sure you'll meet some nice people on your travels."

Again with that! Why didn't people understand? He was a *solo* traveler, he didn't even have a dog. His picture of the desert came to him then, as it regularly did: a vast place of towering rock formations, bare of any vegetation, and from horizon to horizon the color of a ripe blood orange. The idea of the picture was that he was in the middle of it, a romantic figure, an explorer, but while the desert was vivid he could never quite see himself there, though he knew what it *should* look like: the lone, stoic, silent man, gazing into the distance, compass hanging in his hand. Instead he just saw the empty desert.

"It'll be Halloween here," Melanie said. "My twins will be trick-or-treating."

"And it will be getting pretty cold here, too, eh?" he said cheerfully. "Time to bundle up. I'm thinking I'll dip down to the south as I make my escape to the west."

"Escape," she said. "That sounds nice."

"Yes, the winter is pretty brutal in these mountains," he said. "I know these mountains."

"I know them too. Grew up here my whole life."

"Those old folks with their RVs up the road there, they won't be sitting out under their awnings drinking their cheap beer much longer." Here, he thought, was something he and his neighbor would surely agree on. They were both tent-campers, both committed to roughing it. "They'll be snowed in up here, and they'll have to take their televisions inside." Melanie was finished with the dishes, and was staring into the woods; he stared at the trees too, gesturing at them as if they were his audience. "Of course, those rigs have everything, don't they, they're self-sufficient. Electricity, water, propane stoves, microwave ovens—sofas and reclining chairs, king-size beds, washers and dryers. Dishwashers!"—here he indicated her cardboard boxes with a sweep of his hand. "I may be exaggerating, but not much. I've never been inside one, of course. But you can see their frilly curtains hanging in the windows, can't you?"

He fell quiet. He saw the snow, waist-deep below the curtained windows, saw it in drifts over the abandoned picnic tables—it was an ice age, the campers marooned inside their tin cans, trapped until the spring thaw. Dear God, he thought. He must go—he must stop moving fifty miles at a time. He must flee, get far south, far west.

Carlton cleared his throat, gazed deep into the trees. "Terrible to imagine," he said, his voice quavering.

Melanie looked at him. "What's terrible?" she asked. "Frilly curtains at the windows?"

"Winter! Imagine what it will be like out here."

"How long are you going to be hanging around, Carlton?" she said, looking square at him, making him look back at her.

"I, uh. I have to get going soon. I'm not sure, but I need to get out of here."

"Don't forget Halloween," she said, and walked away.

Carlton sat in his chair, with a book unopened on his lap, thinking about the Japanese websites he had seen, and the crazy English translations his computer produced: *Foogle is the special joy! Have fun not touching food!*

He was in his expedition coat, high-tech fleece zipped into a breathable, blizzard-proof shell with lots of little adjustable elastic cords he fiddled with too much, and he also wore a fleece skullcap and fleece gloves with open fingertips that let him do fine-motor tasks with relative ease. The days were getting crisp, the nights genuinely cold, and Carlton expected to leave in another day or two.

Melanie and her children were talking in their tent, and their voices were getting louder. Carlton turned his book over, looked at the cover. It was an old spy thriller he'd read before. It occurred to him, if I'm going to write a book, hadn't I better start taking notes?

"Why do we have to be the same?" the little boy said, in a loud, whining voice. "Why can't I be something else?"

He needed a haircut, Carlton had noticed. Both the

children had bright blond hair, and his was hanging in his eyes.

"Because it's all we have for costumes, these old blue sheets," their mother said. "I don't want to hear it."

"I don't want to be a stupid ghost!"

Carlton imagined Melanie sighing, trying to get the children to stand still, draping them in the sheets.

"Ghosts aren't blue!" said the little girl. "Everybody knows they're white."

"Actually," their mother said, "there are some very special ghosts that are blue. They're real rare. Only one in a million gets to be blue, which is why you don't ever hear about them. The two of you get to be two in two million."

There was silence then, as the children, Carlton assumed, were cooperating.

"Let's go trick or treating!" Melanie said, in a bright, bizarre voice. Parenthood, thought Carlton. No thank you. Embarrassing the things you had to do and say.

There was a lot of shrieking then, and the kids ran out of the tent, which made Carlton look up. The two little ghosts stopped short and stared at him. He had expected them to be completely draped in the sheets, with holes cut out for their eyes, but instead their costumes ended at the neck so their blond heads stuck out. He found this vaguely disappointing.

They stared. They looked like two ghosts who'd seen a ghost. And then they tore off in the opposite direction, up the hill toward the other campers. Melanie shrugged at Carlton, and turned to follow them.

He watched her go. In her puffy jacket, her feminine shape was obscured, but she had the pleasant walk of a woman, an easy roll of the hips. Of course, he wasn't interested in her that way, he wouldn't dream of it, but he counted himself a red-blooded American male and proud of it.

She hurried a little to catch up with her children, and he got up from his chair and stepped out to the road to keep her in view. He moved over to the trees on the other side, so if she turned around he could pretend to be looking at something there. He put a hand out to the twigs of a sapling growing along the edge, and fondled them absent-mindedly. From his place there he could see the first motor home the little family had come to—the children in their shapeless blue gowns fidgeting before the door, where someone he could not see was talking to them. Melanie stood out in the middle of the dirt road, watching.

She lifted a hand to wave at the person who'd come to the door, as her twins ran ahead to the next campsite. They disappeared from view—he couldn't see the next trailer, which was set back a little—but Melanie stayed out in the road. She stirred the gravel with her foot and looked down at it. He wondered what she was thinking. He imagined her smiling as she studied the dirt at her feet, smiling in that way that always looked tired, almost sad. Maybe they could all travel together for a while! It was a crazy thought, but why not? Melanie would probably appreciate the presence of a protective male, journeying, as she was, alone with her two small children. They wouldn't always have to be in campsites that were so close together, either. They could have a little space and privacy, and get together for meals or just to visit. Of course, he didn't know where she was headed, but it didn't matter; his itinerary was open, and he could simply follow her lead for a short while.

Then he remembered how she didn't have a car. He still didn't know what to make of that. No man had shown up, and Carlton had dismissed that possibility—there was no husband, no father, he decided. Maybe the car was in for repairs, and that's why the sister (or whoever she was, but he was pretty sure they were sisters) had said she would return the following week—maybe she would bring the car, or take Melanie to get it. It was a long time to be without your car. But it made sense in a way—if you're stuck without a car for several days or a week, why not go camping? Although perhaps this meant Melanie would be returning home when she had her car again, which would make his idea about them traveling together a non-starter.

He decided, because of this, he would keep the plan to himself. But watching her dawdle up the road behind her children, the idea kept insisting itself. He imagined her in the passenger seat beside him, smiling her weary smile but looking softer, happier, while the children giggled quietly, in the back, behind them. Because she didn't have a car, his imagination jumped to the vision of her riding in his.

"I told that lady I'm a blue ghost!" yelled the little girl. They were heading back toward their campsite. The girl was running in front, zigzagging like a tiny drunk around the potholes, her brother close behind her, their shopping bags swaying but barely slowing them down.

And then they saw Carlton, standing in his arbitrary spot at the side of the road, and they slowed and slumped along, their bags suddenly weighing them down. They stopped at their site, and stood looking at their tent. Their mother trailed them, coming down the road. Carlton crossed, casually, back to his campsite.

Melanie joined her children, and they conferred in soft voices. Carlton, not knowing what to do with himself—it happened a lot when Melanie was around—walked in a circle around his car and sat down in his chair.

"I don't want to!" said the little boy.

"Now, Josh," said his mother, and then spoke too softly to hear.

The next thing Carlton knew the children were standing in front of him, with Melanie behind them, biting her lip.

"Trick or treat!" the children called together, holding out their bags.

"What?" he said.

Melanie's face wore an odd expression, but he couldn't bring himself to look at it. "Trick or treat," repeated the little girl, in a smaller voice.

"I don't have anything," said Carlton. "I had no idea."

"What do you mean?" said Melanie.

He stood up suddenly, which frightened the ghosts, and they backed away, paused, and then fled to their own campsite. Melanie turned to look at them—they milled around for a minute, then settled at the picnic table to examine their loot. "Don't you eat any of that till I get there!" she yelled, with such force that the children sat stock still.

"You!" she hissed at Carlton, trying to keep her voice down.

"I could give them some—instant oatmeal packets," he said.

"I *told* you the other day—I *warned* you so you'd know—"

"Yes—you did—I thought you were warning me to watch out, you know, for teenagers—"

"I told you my kids would be trick or treating."

"Yes, but…"

"But what?"

"I suppose I assumed you'd be taking them somewhere to trick or treat—you know, taking them somewhere."

"This isn't 'somewhere'? This *is* somewhere, dude! Believe it or not, this is somewhere. Everywhere is somewhere for somebody."

What was she talking about? "I know, but I thought you would take them to a neighborhood. Back to where you live or . . ." The fact was, he hadn't thought about it at all, and he had no idea how one trick-or-treated with children.

"When are you leaving, Carlton?"

"In one to two days, probably two."

"Tomorrow or the next day, is that what you mean?"

"Probably the day after tomorrow." He remembered his idea about their traveling together. "But I'm flexible," he added. "I can stay, leave, anytime."

"It's almost winter. It's getting cold here."

"You're right about that!"

"They'll be turning off the water at the spigots soon, and we'll have to carry our water down from the bathrooms."

"I'll be gone by then."

"That's right, you won't be here to help me carry the water. And that will be just too damn bad."

For some reason she was angry. He tried his friendliest smile. "Maybe you should think about moving on too—camping somewhere a little warmer. You don't want your little ones to catch cold."

"What, you think I can't keep them warm?"

"No, I didn't mean that," said Carlton. "I'm sorry—I'm very sorry about the Halloween candy. Really I am." He wasn't used to apologies, and was surprised how warm and pleasant it felt. It was almost as if he were watching himself from the outside, and he cut a very appealing figure. "It looks as if they got plenty of candy from the other campers, though."

"You see those sleeping bags?" said Melanie. She was pointing to the clothes-lines she had strung between the trees on the far side of her campsite, on which she had hung three sleeping bags to air.

"Yes," Carlton said, confused. One of the sleeping bags had pink cartoon mermaids on it, and another had pictures of ducks in green and black and red; they were both small—children's size. The third was larger, in a dull camouflage print.

"Do you notice anything about them?"

"What do you mean? The patterns, the colors?"

"Anything they have in common?"

"No."

"They're summer sleeping bags."

He looked—she was right.

"Lightweight sleeping bags," she said, "for sleep-overs, on other kids' bedroom floors."

He didn't understand. Obviously, he had never noticed or thought about it before, when he'd seen the bags airing on the line.

"You don't get it, do you?" she said.

"Get what?"

"You said we ought to go someplace warmer—" She laughed, but her eyes were not laughing.

"Yes, someplace warmer," said Carlton. Should he—? "Melanie," he said. "I have an idea. If you want to travel somewhere warmer, well, I could, too. What I mean is we could travel together, for company, for a while—you know what I mean?" He shot her a big, neighborly grin.

"What are you—you think—"

"What?"

"You think—oh my God—"

"Oh, no no! Nothing like that! Heavens no!"

Melanie looked over at her children—they sat frozen in their places at the picnic table, wide-eyed.

"I think it's time to move on," Melanie said, in a low voice.

"Yes, we should all get going, as you said, the weather's turning cold—I'm going, and you should go—what I mean is, you should head home or somewhere—I'm so sorry, I never meant to offend you—"

"I don't have a car, Carlton."

"I know."

"Well, if you *know*— Oh, never mind."

"Again, I apologize. I didn't mean anything—"

"I know, I know, all right already."

"And the Halloween candy too, I'm sorry about that."

"I know."

"We'll keep a sharp lookout tonight, for any pranksters."

"You are unreal."

She turned away, began to walk to her picnic table. Carlton felt badly, though he thought she had overreacted somewhat. He considered this possibility of Halloween pranks—it was just afternoon, the light starting to slant through the trees, and those teenagers might come around when it got dark. It made him uncomfortable, and protective of Melanie too—they might throw eggs at her tent, or something equally bad.

"I'll keep an eye out," he called to her. "I'll run off any intruders."

"What does he mean, Mommy?" he heard the little girl say.

"He doesn't mean nothing," her mother answered. "He's crazy, don't you pay any attention to him."

That night Carlton Deming slept and dreamed, but did not dream of Halloween hooligans. He dreamed of elderly RV-campers trapped inside a television set, knocking on the glass to get out. He dreamed of his long-dead father, who was laughing, very amused about something, and other people appeared then, all around—Adams and Mary Gunther and the others. He hated sleeping, because he hated dreaming.

In the very early morning, before it got light, Melanie Dabney was in the deep sleep of real forgetting and did not stir as Carlton moved around outside. When he pulled his first tent stake out of the ground—in the dark, doing it by feel—he remembered he had just dreamed the opposite: pounding a stake into the dirt, though he couldn't recall the rest.

When his car started up and pulled quietly away, it stirred Melanie enough to make her dream it was her sister's car, driving away from the campsite.

And then she dreamed she was explaining to her mother, who in reality had died a decade before, everything that had happened to her in the last year. And then she was lying on a carpet, looking out a small window, through thin cotton curtains to a blue sky. Her children, curled like kittens against her, both burrowed closer at that moment, a stimulus that emptied her sleep of its dream.

As Carlton crept up the road, rocking through the potholes, passing the dark RVs on both sides, he thought of the slumbering, open-mouth-breathing old crones all around him, passing another night waiting for death in their tin can slums, and he thought, no, not him, nosirree, he was not waiting for death, it would have to come find him. He dropped his registration in the after-hours box at the top of the road, thinking, they can keep the extra money, it wasn't much anyway. I could write a book, he reminded himself: *Campgrounds I Have Known.* Dear God, *this* place! He preferred state parks, they were so—public, so nonprofit, so park-like. But this place, *this* was not his idea of a campground, God no.

It was high time he got out of there. High time, high time. He knew when he wasn't wanted.

The last thing he remembered of the place, as he turned onto the paved road—and then, he felt sure, he would put it out of his mind, and move on—was standing in the dark, leaning over Melanie's picnic table, keeping the flashlight away from her tent; he remembered how he'd added, on impulse, another zero to the number on the check. He slipped the end of the check under the corner of her pots-and-pans box. He turned off his flashlight and stood there, waiting for his eyes to get used to the dark. He imagined her standing in front of him, holding open a big bag and saying *trick or treat* with that familiar, odd smile on her face, and when he dropped the check in her bag, her smile stayed sad and hard.

He drove into the grainy, soft lightening of dawn. The woods all around were beginning to emerge, slowly, out of the night. He wondered how things were going in Japan. *Foogle makes happy parents and children mostly!* He went slowly up the winding mountain road, toward a state park he had picked out forty-five miles away, a little to the east, and a little to the north.

Rapture

Good writers borrow; great writers steal.
—never said by T.S. Eliot

This one wasn't like the others, not like that insurance salesman who said, I really like your living room, let's go back out to your living room. Or the computer geek who gulped and blinked the whole time he was in there. Worst of all was the black-leather motorcycle guy who staggered around laughing and said, oh man, is it okay if I light up a joint in here? He lost all interest in her and sat huddled on the bed, smoking and staring.

You should not think that Marina was screwing lots of guys all the time. These few encounters stretched over a ten-year period between her twenty-fifth and thirty-fifth birthdays, during which time her peculiar project was evolving, ferociously.

This new man, Rock, was different. He whirled around, arms outstretched, like some beautiful ballet dancer, and he came to rest with a look of pure delight on his face. He was, as well, the best-looking man she'd found. He was lean and tall and wore skintight jeans and a white tee shirt that stretched armpit to armpit across his pectoral muscles. His face looked carved out of stone, his eyes were deep and brown, and he had lovely, shaggy hair. He looked, she thought, like the early Bruce Springsteen.

He locked his eyes onto hers, an open-mouth smile, the shape of a laugh, playing on his face.

What do you call it? he asked.

He meant the fishnets draped along the walls, the floats and crab traps hanging from them; the myriad shells and chunks of coral stuck to the ceiling, arranged in baskets, glued into sculptures; the pictures of lighthouses and sailboats and storms at sea; the fishtank with the artificial fish; the models of clipper ships, some of them inside bottles and some of them not; the inflatable mermaid; the rather large papier mâché submarine; the dolphins at play in the surf; the anchors and the block and tackle and the semaphore flags; the barometer in the shape of a ship's wheel; the dried starfishes; the driftwood; the life preservers; the *Welcome Aboard* sign; the ship's clock; the ship's bell; the oars; the compass; the diver down flag; the seafoam carpet and the coordinating curtains with their light, feminine seashell-and-fish design; the bedspread, of course, with its rather bolder nautical motif, all ropes and anchors intertwined; and all the rest.

Rapture of the Deep, she replied.

And he took her in his arms and they fell together onto her big bed and they went at it with a fury unlike anything she'd ever known.

It was love.

♪

Rock had recently become a musician. Previously he had been a seller of roses on the shoulder of the road, and before that a telephone service entrepreneur, calling people at the dinner hour from his home until that got old. And before that he'd been an employee at several fast food franchises in succession, leaving each when the smells got to him, trading them in each time for a new set of smells until all of it started to smell the same, and then he knew he had to get out completely. Selling roses had been tolerable at first. How romantic, she told him. She imagined him standing there, rugged, alone, his eyes staring into the distance (to where the cars topped the hill), clutching the long-stemmed bouquet to his bold breast. It was okay, he said, except when it rained. Then you got soaked and nobody stopped. People only want roses on nice days. It was a bad gig in winter. And it got really, really boring after a while.

So now he was going to be a rock star, he hoped. How did you learn to play the guitar so quickly? she wanted to know. He only had to master a few chords, he said, shrugging. And sing. His voice didn't have to be that great, because all the music his band made got re-distorted electronically. The driving force behind this band was not a musician at all, did not play with the band except in the sense that he played, radically and endlessly, with the tapes that they made. Marina wasn't sure she understood. It was a kind of techno-grunge-dance-rap music, he explained. White boy punk-techno-hiphop. Cutting edge stuff. Marina was impressed. You like that kind of music? she asked. Not really, he said. Then he amended that, saying that, yeah, he liked it, he liked all kinds of music, that it didn't really matter because the main thing was that this was the vehicle for his art.

The vehicle for your art? Marina said. She was a dental hygienist, having become one because her mother was a dental hygienist.

I am a songwriter, he said.

What do you write about?

Everything. Food, the weather, love, sex, being broke, clothing, death.

Wow.

That's the main thing I do for the band. They could get anybody to do the singing and play the guitar, especially since it doesn't come out sounding the way it goes in. There's just one little problem that's bugging me.

What's that?

When Fred gets done with it (Fred's the guy who mixes the music), you can't hear the lyrics. I don't care that it doesn't sound like singing, but you can't hear any of the words. I don't think you need to hear all of them, just some of them. But I have to stay cool, because this is my ticket out of poverty.

You look like one of those One Direction guys. I don't know their names.

I do not! he said. He pulled his hand from her breast, rolled back on his back, stared at a fish on the ceiling. I'm an original! he said. I'm not an imitation!

I didn't mean that, she protested. Oh, it hurt her so that she had hurt him. She vowed never to do anything stupid again. Artists are temperamental, she reminded herself. Besides, he didn't really look like that One Direction guy. He looked more like a cross between Adam Levine and Enrique Iglesias. And maybe Sting when Sting was much, much younger.

♪

The friction between them did not last long. She smoothed it over with kisses. It did disturb her, a little, sometimes, that he could be testy like that, and other things as well—suddenly distant, perhaps preoccupied with a difficult song lyric (there's times they just don't come out right, he told her), and forgetful, impulsive, easily distracted. But he was tender and sweet too. They could lie for hours together, talking, not talking, cuddling, and he seemed to like it as much as she did. He would ask her about the stuff on the walls, where the different things came from, how she decided what went where. She realized it had come about organically—that was the word she stumbled upon, surprised and impressed with herself as its syllables passed her lips.

Organically, he said. Wow.

She told him how with each addition (and there were still things she added, little things, all the time) she would stand in the middle of her room and turn slowly around, holding the object in her hands, feeling its weight and shape, just looking at everything until it came to her, where the new piece ought to go. She rarely moved anything around; once something found its place that's where it seemed to belong.

It's intuitive, she said, another word that rather astonished her, a pretty word, she thought. These words seemed to come from the same place the arrangement on her walls came from—from Inspiration.

But there was a science to it too. There were rules. She told him about how, for instance, seagulls were Rapture but geese were not. It could get tricky. Juxtapositions were important (though she did not know this word—instead she spoke of putting odd things side by side). You could not have a lot of fish and shells together in a clump, nor could you group together too much boating paraphernalia—the idea was to have, say, a marlin leaping over a porthole, over top of a picture of some dunes, above a few crab floats arranged on the floor. It was only in talking about it that she discovered all this. Rock listened, really listened. Sometimes he was remarkably good at that. He spoke, almost grandly but with a bit of a reverent hush too, of the West Wall, the East Wall. He referred to the Ceiling of the Sistine/Aquamarine Chapel.

I love your room, he said. It's so unique. Like our love. He suggested she get some fishnet stockings.

She was thrilled to think she was an inspiration for his work. She thought, maybe he will write a song about my bedroom, but she didn't mention this because if it did happen she wanted him to come up with it on his own. When she was alone in her room, she looked at her surroundings in a new way. It was because of him, she knew. She looked at everything, saw the rhythms in it, the order, the cleverness. She thought, I am an artist too.

She went to her mirror, which was large and round, framed by a ship's wheel with dried seaweed hanging on the spokes. She saw the usual face, the one she'd seen too many times to ever see it new, her face which aged all the time, she knew, degree by degree, imperceptibly but nonetheless. Sometimes she caught up with this difference, or it caught up with her, and she saw something there—a line, a settling—she hadn't seen before. This was such a moment. How long—? she thought, scrutinizing the mature, deep look of her hazel eyes. Her fine brown, limp hair still hung around her face like a girl's. Her mouth wore a baby pout. But her eyes kept coming back to her eyes. I've changed, she thought.

I want Rock to write a song about me, she thought—which is exactly what he did.

♫

I want to play something for you, he said. He took her hand and led her into the bedroom, his Stratocaster under his other arm. She thought, could this be—?

Wait till you hear this, he said. It's inspired, he said.

He sat cross-legged on the bed and began strumming on his guitar, though it didn't make a real full noise because it wasn't plugged in. Then he started singing.

step into my fuck-palace
said the spider to the fly
when I went into her bedroom
it made me want to cry

What! said Marina. She was about to say more, but Rock continued strumming.

step into my fuck-palace
said the spider to the fly
when I went—

Wait! said Marina. That's the same verse.

Yeah, well, I only need one verse. That's all Fred needs to work with.

What's that supposed to mean—'It made me want to cry'? That sounds bad.

Well, like, it means cry for joy—it made me want to cry for joy.

It doesn't sound like that.

Don't worry anyway. By the time Fred gets through with it the words will be all gone. Although I've been working on him, lately, to keep some of the words legible. He says he will, for the right song. What do you think of that? Maybe this will be the right song.

She didn't know what to think of that. She went to the Goodwill store to make herself feel better, where she found a nice ashtray that said "Salty Seadog" on it and had a sailor's head, with a funny hat and a big pipe, sticking up at one end. She filled the ashtray with sand, in which she planted stubs of dry coral like cigarette butts.

♫

Fred doesn't like the song, he said. I'm not surprised, she thought. He sat on the floor of her room, sulking, idly twirling the frayed ends of a piece of old hemp rope that hung over the side of her dressing table.

She tried to change the subject. She pointed out her latest acquisitions. She talked about how her bedroom gave her something to do. She haunted yard sales and thrift shops, she explained, where these sorts of items could always be counted on to turn up. Everybody goes to the beach and buys something, she said, oh, you know, like a shell with a picture of a lighthouse painted on it, and five years later finds it in the basement and wonders whatever possessed them to buy such a thing.

Yeah, he said.

Beach vacations and such are happy times, she said. The objects are infused with the happiness spirit. At the same time, though, people don't invest too much of themselves in them, don't become overly attached, so that these things keep a kind of anonymity, a universality even. From a practical point of view, it means people are easily parted from them, so that they fall that much more easily into my hands.

Rock didn't say anything.

It's inspired, she said.

Yes, inspired, he said, not sounding very inspired.

They are orphans. I give them back the love they knew when their owners first found them and responded, irrationally, to that giddy impulse to buy them.

I'm going to write another song, said Rock, staring at his shoes. I better go talk to Fred, he said, standing up.

I am the ultimate beachcomber! she said.

♪

Marina felt lonely sometimes when she was all by herself in her room. The decor was meant to keep her company—it was the noisiest room in town—but sometimes it was deathly quiet in there. She saw ghosts: the ghosts of fishermen who not longer put to sea, the ghosts of shipwrecked sailors. The ghosts of everyone else's summer vacations.

She had bought this house, and begun this project, a long time ago, and she cried now because of the broken heart that had caused her to buy the house in the first place. She had failed to realize she was buying the house too soon, before her heart had a chance to mend. Too soon, too soon, she thought, but so much time had passed now. She wasn't sure it ever would mend, now that she had taken up with this young musician.

Because she always wore her emotions just under the surface, something as simple as looking at two seahorses kissing on the wall could make her cry.

♪

Marina!

It was Rock, on the phone.

Listen! I wrote a new song! Fred says it's the one!

You mean he'll make the lyrics so you can hear them?

Not just that. He says this is the *one*—he knows a guy—he says he can get us a contract, a big music deal. Fred's mixing the song a whole new way. Fred says—

This Fred has altogether too weird a grip on you.

There's nothing sexual between me and Fred.
Good grief, I didn't say there was.
You haven't met Fred, have you?
What do you know about this record contract?
Listen, listen!
What choice did she have but to listen? She stood with the phone against her ear. Listen! he said.
There was a nervous thrill to his voice as he began, a quality Marina hadn't heard before. His voice came through the phone line tinny and harsh, the barely discernible plucking of guitar strings in the background. Like a really bad recording made in somebody's garage, which was, as it happened, precisely the setting Fred used to do his work.
> *rapture rapture rapture of the deep*
> *rapture rap-rap-rap-rapture*
> *I couldn't get a wink of sleep*

What do you think?
Gee, I don't know. I guess I'd have to hear a little more.
I don't have any more, not just yet, but I'm going to write more. I have a little stuff, I haven't put it together yet—
> *crab trap and net and everything wet*
> *that's what this little girl's room is made of*
> *waves and shells and fishing boat smells . . .*

Gee, Rock, it's real inventive, but—
Wait—
> *she looked so cute*
> *in her mermaid suit—*

Enough. I've heard enough.
It's genius! Pure genius!
But whose genius, was what Marina was thinking.

♪

Marina was sitting on her bed leafing through an old issue of *Skin Diver* when the phone rang. She knew it was Rock. He didn't come over anymore, he was too busy, but he kept calling her. Her bedroom telephone resembled a sunken treasure chest—when she lifted the barnacle-encrusted, gilt lid (the receiver) to her ear, a heap of gleaming pieces of eight and Spanish doubloons was revealed inside.

She heard Rock rattling on, something about Hollywood and fame and fortune, but she was more interested in admiring the silk nightie she was wearing, a short little pastel number with an impressionistic seashell design, tiny straps, and padded cups for her breasts like two scallop shells. It was only lately that she'd started to seek out and buy Rapture lingerie. She heard Rock say he'd written some more verses for his song. She spontaneously composed a little ditty of her own:
I like silk nighties
Yes I do
I like silk nighties
Better than you
You haven't heard a word I've said, said Rock.
Of course I have.
I just said, I'm flying to L.A. this afternoon.
Um, yes—
We finished the tape, it's got a whole new sound. That Fred is a genius—
Look, Rock—
If I make it in L.A. I'm gonna have Fred to thank—
Now, hold up. Listen. Your song—I have to tell you this—you need to be concerned about this. Your song is a rip-off.
What? You're crazy. You've never heard a song like this song.
I beg to differ. Did you ever hear "Ducks on the Wall" by the Kinks?
I—don't know.
It goes *You're so hot, but I can't ball, 'cause of those ducks on your bedroom wall*, or something like that.
That's ridiculous. My song is not about ducks.

Or maybe it's *I wanna ball, but those ducks on your wall are scaring me*—wait a minute, that doesn't even rhyme, but anyway I can't remember, and probably that's good because if you quote things without permission you can get sued.

Whatever. Your stupid duck song has nothing to do with me. Look, I got a plane to catch.

I'm trying to talk to you!

I think you're jealous, that's what I think.

Oh yeah? Well, you're ripping off my room, that's what I think!

Your room! A second ago I was ripping off the Kinks! How can I be ripping off your room if I'm ripping off the Kinks?

See, you admit it.

I admit nothing. I'm just saying.

You're ripping off my room!

Well, you ripped your room off somebody else!

WHAT!

You didn't think I knew, did you? That little cartoon in the corner, next to the anchor? That you got from that book called *Sailing*?

I've got *three* books called *Sailing*, spread around my room! Or maybe you didn't notice!

It's the cartoon book—

By Beard and McKie—

Who cares. The point is I know your dirty little secret! You Xeroxed that cartoon right out of that book, it's a picture of all that—stuff—and it says "Rapture of the Deep" right in the corner!

My room is an original! It goes way, way beyond that cartoon. That cartoon is simply one more item, among hundreds—a single brush-stroke upon the canvas of my room.

Admit it! You stole the idea!

You stole the idea!

I am an original! You are an imitation! Even your name—Marina—it means *dock*, it means *yacht club.*

It's an old Russian family name!

From some old Russian boatyard.

And what kind of a fucking name is Rock? A chunk of fucking concrete. And your band, your band doesn't even have a name!

Oh, yes it does! The Bottom Feeders!

I'll get you back for this.

You don't have a patent on your fucking decor. You can't copyright fucking seashells and stinky old fishnets and all that crap!

Crap!?

Yes. Crap.

♪

To make a long story short, Rock went out to California and became a pop music star. Marina called him a couple times, calls he did not return. She decided to try to track down Fred, which turned out to be easy. He immediately agreed to meet her, as soon as she told him who she was.

They met at a smoky, sleepy, vinyl-and-velvet cocktail lounge that was Fred's idea. It was the middle of the afternoon, a brilliantly sunny day outside, so that when she walked into the bar she felt blind and had to stand there what seemed a long time, looking around, waiting for her eyes to adjust. As she stood there she realized she had no way of recognizing Fred, except by his voice, which matched, strangely, the dim, dust-laden sultriness of this place. But when she saw him alone at the bar, she knew it was him.

It was his voice all right as he returned her greeting and lifted his long fingers from his swizzle stick to shake her hand. He had a glass of weird-looking green stuff over ice.

What are you drinking? she asked, glancing around for the bartender. Fred responded with a throaty, gothic-horror kind of laugh.

Anisette, he said. Or is this ouzo, or Pernod? I forget. Because absinthe is illegal, you know.

Oh, brother, thought Marina, obviously someone here was born at the wrong time.

He looked like a cross between Prince and Michael Jackson—Prince the way he looked before he tried to take his real name back and Michael Jackson way back around the time he married Lisa Marie Presley. He wore a velvet bell-bottom jumpsuit and platform shoes. He had skin like slick, pale dead fish skin, and black wavy hair that was short at the sides but came down in the back over his collar, and a faint mustache that looked as if it was trying very hard to grow.

What do you hear from Rock? he asked, dripping-sweet. She couldn't read that—whether there was an edge there or not.

Well, that's the thing. I don't hear from him. I thought maybe you could tell me what he was up to.

HA! he shouted, hurting her ear. He'd evidently had a few of these anisettes, or ouzos, or Pernods already. Our young friend has flown the coop! Gone undercover! Incognito!

Hardly incognito, said Marina. His face is on all the teen fanzines. I saw them at the Barnes & Noble—you look up at the magazine rack and there he is, staring down at you, all hungry and hot, from a dozen different vantage points.

A dozen perches! Perched up there like a goddamn parrot.

Or a buzzard, said Marina.

Not to mention I saw him at the supermarket. I was just trying to buy some weenies and milk and a candy bar and I look up from the line and there's his airbrushed face grinning right at me. He's got an earring now.

You mean you're not—producing him—anymore?

Hell no! I gave his tape to a friend of a friend, who introduced him to another friend who got him signed with some big production company and that's the last I saw of Rock. Ungrateful little bastard. I made him! I gave him his sound! He had the looks, but it was *my* tape.

Fred stirred his green drink furiously.

You know who I am, don't you? Marina asked.

Of course. You're the girl with the wonderful bedroom.

What are we going to do, Fred?

Nothing we can do. I already talked to a lawyer.

There's other ways we can get him back.

Nothing that isn't illegal or dangerous or both. I am not a criminal. I will not sink to his level.

I'm thinking we go public. Come out with an exposé. Tell our side of the story.

No one's going to be interested in that. He's America's darling. It would be different if he were some sleazy old actor screwing around on the set, some jaded jetsetter working on his fifth wife. But nobody's going to want to burst the bubble of all those eleven-year-old girls who sleep with his poster staring down at their bed.

Surely Americans are hungry for any kind of scandal?

You underestimate his handlers. He's new, he's hot. They're not going to let the likes of you and me rock the boat. Ha! That was funny, get it? *Rock*—the *boat*.

Maybe you're right.

Take it from me, you ought to just curl up with your stuffed porpoises or whatever it is you've got and just be glad you have them and forget about Rock.

I'm so pissed off at him.

He stole your heart, sweetie, but he stole a lot more than that from me.

It's not that, said Marina, grabbing his arm to get his attention. He stole my ideas, Fred. He stole my *room*.

Fred looked at her, blinking in surprise. Marina realized it was only now dawning on him what her investment was in all this.

Oh, said Fred. He probably would have been more articulate had he been sober. He started to insert a pale finger up his nose until he noticed Marina noticing this.

Oh, well, fuck it, said Marina.

I would really like to see your room some time, said Fred. He blinked at her, this time not in a surprised but in a smiling kind of way. She couldn't tell what that was about—was he just being friendly, or what? She glanced down at the pale skin of his meatless chest, where it disappeared below the deep V-collar of his jumpsuit. I've heard so much about it, he added. The undersea motif.

Rapture of the Deep, she corrected.

Of course.

♫

Marina made frequent, small trips to the supermarket, rather than buying her groceries all at once, and she found excuses to go to Walmart where they had a magazine rack in the bookstore section. She monitored every imaginable print source for news of Rock, and he was all over the internet, but she quit looking for him online after she found a Rapture of the Deep website one day and nearly burst into tears—she had clicked on a link and suddenly found herself in an intricate maze of swimming fishes blowing bubbles and sailing ships drifting by and whales spouting and crabs dancing—the graphics astonished and upset her, it was so much more than what she could do and, at the same time, wrong.

She found Rock in *Us, People, Seventeen, Time,* and *Rolling Stone.* And there were all the teeny-bop fan magazines, of course, but these she grew bored with after a while, their coverage was so thin and saccharine.

She studied the pictures for clues. She was angered to see, sometimes, nautical backdrops featured in the posed shots. One full-page portrait, in *Entertainment,* displayed him sitting on a hunk of coral with scepter and pitchfork, like Neptune. She had to admit, that one was pretty clever, and for a fleeting moment she forgot her bitterness, caught by the old enchantment, by the come-hither look in his twinkly, brown, laughing eyes that seemed meant for her only, reaching to her from across the barrier of the hard, shiny ink of the magazine page. But then she saw he was two-dimensional, that she could move the paper and his image would bend and roll around and his eyes would stare at the ceiling or the wall, and that she could turn the page and make him disappear.

Marina called *People* and got transferred to the voicemail of the person who'd been writing their pieces on the Bottom Feeders, a certain Preston Lacrouche. She left an urgent message. When Lacrouche did not call her back, she emailed:

>Dear Mr. Lacrouche,
>I know you have been following the career antics of Rock Lobster and the Bottom Feeders, but I have information that may be of interest to you, concerning the moral character and behavior of Mr. Lobster. I have evidence that he has stolen material from other artists. I am anxious to share my discoveries with you at your earliest convenience.

An email came back which said:

>Thank you for contacting us. Rock Lobster is an exciting new talent who is taking the music world by storm! I can assure you you'll be seeing more of this bright young star in our pages. So keep watching!

Marina replied:

>You don't get it. Rock Lobster is a crook and I have proof. Aren't you interested in this?

Nothing came back after that.

♪

Marina and Fred sat at a McDonalds together having lunch. They were both eating Chicken McNuggets because there was a promotional on and the nuggets were about half their usual price. Marina had insisted he meet her so she could update him.

She shifted her rear end on the hard plastic chair. Here's a thought, she said. There's that old song "Rock Lobster" by The B-52s. Wouldn't Rock be familiar with that song?

Maybe, maybe not, said Fred. In any case I don't think you could get him on that. A lobster is just a crustacean. It's not like anybody invented it.

People magazine will probably sue me, she said, when they find out the terrible things I've been saying about them. I've got this idea I'm gonna tell *Us* everything, including the cold shoulder I got at *People*, and then *People* is gonna read about it in *Us* and I'm gonna be in a whole lot of trouble.

But don't you have a certain amount of literary license? asked Fred. If everything's said in a spirit of fun?

Fun? This isn't fun! My honor is at stake. This is about honor, character, integrity!

You'll forgive me, but I think the oakum between your planks is a little loose, girl.

This is a battle to the death, all-out war. I will prevail.

When you shake your head, do you hear loose coral rattling around in there?

I can't believe you don't want to screw this guy, too.

Screw this guy . . . my dear Marina—

You know what I mean. Screw him to the wall.

Hmm. Well, yes. I do regret—

So you're with me on this?

You know what? Fred said, turning a bitten chicken nugget in his hand. I think they bleach the dark meat in these to make it white.

Wouldn't they have to say if they did that?

I don't know. You know, Marina, I just don't know anymore. I don't know what they tell us and what they don't.

They stood up to go. Lighten up, girl, said Fred.

Marina grunted. Fred flashed her a thin-lipped, toothy grin. He wrapped his long pale fingers around her pink hands.

Smiles are free, he said, so give generously.

Smiles are precious, Marina replied. Spend wisely.

♪

Marina was unhappy with Fred's lukewarm response. How could someone so grievously wronged be so blasé? She went from McDonalds to the Barnes & Noble across the parking lot, and headed upstairs to the CD section where she started flipping, mindlessly at first, through the plastic cases until she found bands with names like Leftover Salmon, Monsters from the Surf, the Oyster Boys. She realized, it might just be her. In the same way, she reflected, that when you buy a new car you start seeing that same model on the highway everywhere you go, so she might be noticing, selectively, copycat Rapture bands, or what she thought anyway were copycat Rapture bands.

She started to leave, and as she reached the top of the stairs she saw something she hadn't seen on the way in. Facing the shoppers as they started downstairs was a life-size cardboard Rock in the tiniest possible bikini swim trunks and nothing else except for flippers on his feet. His hair was wet and tossed. There were little beads of water on his skin that she knew were fake because the photographer's lights would dry those up in a heartbeat. It seemed he had a new album: *Tsunami of Love*.

Maybe Fred was right. You couldn't stop a tidal wave. A lone voice crying in the wilderness of publicity would never be heard. She should give it up and move on with her life, whatever that was.

She went back to her room and sat on the bed, trying to draw comfort from the walls. She gazed into the busy, busy decor; her eyes blurred, she lost herself there, but she didn't really feel any better. Her focus sharpened again and she noticed that the spot where she was staring was entirely filled up—no room for another single thing! Before long it would all be that way, and what would she do then? When her Rapture was complete, would her ocean overflow? Would it spill down the hall, into the bathroom, the kitchen? No, that wasn't how it was supposed to be. She couldn't bear to think of it, to think of the future. The only thing she was sure of, she decided, was that she would never, never be so foolish again, never again share with any man her secret joys.

She stopped watching magazine covers, changed the settings on her car radio all to classical stations, and stayed away from the bookstore entirely.

And then one day there was a message on her telephone answering machine, an unfamiliar woman's voice, identifying herself as Preston Lacrouche, requesting Marina call her back as soon as possible.

Lacrouche is a woman! thought Marina. More to the point, why is she calling me? This time Lacrouche was readily accessible by phone. Marina learned that Mr. Lobster had been caught in a car with an underage girl ho hum couldn't he think of something a bit more original? The discovery happened in the girl's driveway and her father was the one who discovered them and took pictures which he sold to *TMZ*. They were calling it 'the capture of Captain Rapture.'

Marina told Lacrouche everything she knew.

♪

It was a weekday but Marina called in sick, inasmuch as dental hygiene held little appeal for her at the moment. The camera crew arrived and spent seeming hours getting the lighting right, intent as they were on bringing out all the color and texture of her bedroom walls, while Ms. Lacrouche interviewed Marina and Fred. The article would quote Marina this way:

> "It's true, you can't copyright a room but there's a basic question of right and wrong here. . . . In a broad sense, I see this as a matter of intellectual property rights. . . . Is this really somebody we want to hold up as some kind of role model for our youth?"

The article would quote Rock's famous song, too.
> *rapture rapture rapture of the deep*
> *all I saw were sharks when I tried to count sheep*
> "Nine- and ten-year-olds are bopping to this song all over the country, but it really has some very adult content, and they don't realize it. I'm not pro-censorship, but it's just another thing that makes me question Rock Lobster's ethics."

The article would also talk about the agreement Marina had reached with her producer, who happened to be (get this!) the same producer who'd given Rock Lobster his start. She was preparing to record an album of her own.

"More of a country sound," Fred would be quoted as saying. "Which is what I'm more interested in now."

Finally the photographers were ready. *People* would end up using a large photo of Marina and Fred sitting on her bed, taken with a wide angle, fisheye lens so that all the stuff on the walls got sucked into the picture. It was shot from floor level so their legs and feet looked big and their heads looked small. Fred's velvet bell-bottom lay over Marina's bare, mini-skirted leg, and tickled.

She was warned to sit still while they got ready for more pictures. She didn't mind, she had waited this long, she could wait a little more. We reap what we sow, she reflected. Hoisted on his own petard, she thought. Where's that from? she wondered. What's a petard?

She began to feel rather philosophical about everything. She sat there pondering the mysterious tidal surges of the heart, the unfathomable currents of one's deep, interior ocean, how things had a way of washing up on the beach and lying there, drying in the sun.

Life's happiness, such as it is, she thought, comes to us in pieces, like the objects on my walls, like a crazy mosaic of all the wrong things that somehow go together and produce the right thing.

An octopus in the corner smiled at her. She smiled back.

"The title cut is bound to be a hit," the article would proclaim, and it would go on to include a few lines that Marina had sung for Preston Lacrouche and the photographers.

Starfish and fishes,
salt and sand and wind and wishes,
I should have known from the start
you'd steal the song from my heart

"Kind of acoustic, folksy," Fred would be quoted as saying.

Marina nodded. "Kind of like Emmylou."

♪

Lola

Lola was a person whose mind wandered a good deal, both when it mattered and when it didn't. Making love with her boyfriend she drifted to the pattern on the pillowcase, which reminded her of the kitchen towels she'd almost bought—those had been pretty, all flowered, too—but she had given up on the idea because she didn't need them and she did not earn the kind of money that could justify such impulses. Not when there were things she truly needed, like pantyhose and postage stamps.

Her wanderings were not always so far off the point. Making love with George she remembered his coy insistence, long ago now, that they could not have intercourse because she was too short. Five-foot-two had been his minimum on account of his being tall—how tall exactly she was not sure—and she was just five-one-and-a-half and perhaps shrinking. In bed with him now, she recalled this height business, the electricity between them when he'd teased her about it, her determination to show him his mistake. It reminded her of those amusement park attractions, the ones with the signs that say *you must be this tall to ride*, which in turn reminded her of her last experience at one of those places, taking her nephew up in that swinging upside-down thing which she hadn't realized swung all the way upside-down and hung there like that, over and over, and her nephew complaining more and more that he was going to be sick, while she tried to reassure him though she was feeling queasy herself mostly because he kept talking about it. She said, close your eyes and try not to think about it—stupid advice but she didn't know what else to say—she knew, even as she said it, how unhelpful it was, and she wondered if she would be any good at all at motherhood or if she would tend, if she had children of her own, always to say the wrong thing. And then, just as George reached orgasm, she saw her nephew throw up, hanging upside down, so that his vomit seemed to fly upward from his head, disappearing above him.

There was one other way in which Lola's mind had a tendency to wander. Sometimes an image would pop into her thoughts, and she would not know where it came from. Not that it came out of nowhere. Rather, these images were haunted by two possibilities—either they had really happened, she had really seen them and had merely forgotten them, or she had dreamed them, last night or, less likely, the night before. It bothered her not to understand their source, and she tended to turn these things over and over in her mind, with the effect that she was distracted from whatever she was meant to be doing at the time.

An example: her boyfriend has rolled away from her and has begun to snore. Suddenly, she sees quite clearly a long-fingered hand, incredibly long fingers wrapped around the neck of a guitar.

Lola first met George one day about a year before, over brown bag lunches on the patio outside the building where they both worked. She was a temp-turned-permanent in the office of a thriving family practice recently made more thriving by merging with another practice—they had asked her to stay on in the chaos of the merger, and she agreed, and continued to file and answer phones and make computer entries and fax results to different places. George worked in an office on the same floor but far down the other end of the building so that a different set of elevators took people to it and away from it again. He was a financial guy there. She thought this meant he was an accountant, but he preferred to refer to himself as a financial guy, so she accepted this, especially since she didn't have a job title of her own, or even words to describe her job to herself.

They had been dating all this time and had not spoken of marriage or even spoken around the edges of it, in part because Lola felt sure that she'd lost her last boyfriend by speaking of marriage too much and too soon. Her mother, she thought, had lost her second husband that way, by being demanding and claustrophobic about marriage, though he had married her, had proceeded that far without complaint, and the problems only began afterward. Commitment terrified Lola, not for the same reasons it scared people like her mother's ex-husband, but because it had the power to chase men away.

At work she was too busy to think about such things. She sat at her desk, the telephone cradled against her ear, listening passively to the woman on the other end, who had a problem Lola would solve for her if she ever stopped talking. She looked up to see a man backing out through the waiting room door, waving goodbye to someone else there as he went. Her mother had taught her, always wave at the mailman, always wave at the guy in the caboose. She imagined, or remembered, the tail end of a train, receding around a gentle curve in the tracks. The smoke it made trailing into smaller puffs, the mechanical sound of it diminishing, diminishing. Had she dreamed this? Seen it on television? The woman on the phone was waiting for her answer; Lola couldn't remember the question. The woman on the phone hissed a loud sigh into Lola's ear.

The day she met George might just as easily have turned out differently. She sat on a bench with her girlfriend, out on the patio at work, munching by turns on each of the items she had assembled around her, sandwich and chips to her left, carrot sticks to her right. She tried not to move much, afraid the splinters of the bench would snag her dress. Everything was in easy reach. She reached, she chewed, she talked to her friend. The benches were arranged in a square, facing in, as if around a fountain or statue that wasn't there; the arrangement always disturbed her. One had to face the people on the bench directly across, who were too close to ignore but too far away to include, casually, in conversation. She did not think it bothered others, but it bothered her. But there was nowhere else outside to go to eat.

Her girlfriend, who was pregnant, was suffering from morning sickness and excused herself. Lola's brown paper lunch bag rested near her, and she studied it—an old one, reused and reused, crumply all over and with a natural curl to the top that fit her hand when she carried it. Something made her look up and fix her eye directly on the lunch bag of the person on the bench across from her; it had the same network of tiny veins—the look of worn brown paper—and a rolled-over top that sort of smiled at her.

And then she did the first thing that was bound to make him think she was peculiar.

She giggled, and quickly brought an embarrassed hand to her mouth, and then she pointed at his lunch bag, and giggled again.

"Hmm?" he said.

"I'm sorry," she said. He waited.

"My lunch . . . ?" he said.

"Your lunch . . . *bag*," she said, "is, is just like mine." She blushed, embarrassed.

His eyes went from her bag to his, to hers again.

He looked into the branches of a Bradford pear at the patio's edge, looked up at the sky, at the small white clouds against the blue. He crossed his legs. He crossed his arms.

"So what did you have for lunch?" he asked, though everything still lay in plain view around her, the half-eaten sandwich, the dwindling carrot sticks.

It might never have happened, had her girlfriend not been pregnant, had there been other people on other benches, had the day not been fine. Or if she, or George, had ordered out at the sub shop that day.

Over the past year they had viewed many movies together and shared many restaurant meals, although lately the meals tended to be more modest and hurried, mostly quick, filling dinners on the way to the movie. They'd gone to her mother's together on Easter Sunday, where they had ham and lemonade at brunch. Her mother lived in a condominium where she always kept the thermostat turned up high; Lola warned George to dress in layers. The place was filled with photographs of Lola and her brothers at every age, and of her mother's sisters and cousins, but no husbands, no fathers. Lola's mother had a huge smile, the product of her perfect dentures.

Lola and George had attended together the confirmation of George's little brother, a lavish affair centered around a compact horde of awkward boys all wearing buttonhole white carnations. There were no girls, it was an all-boys school. Lola smiled politely the entire time, sure that George's family was watching her.

Afterwards, though, making her goodbyes to George's parents, she lost her smile briefly, distracted by an image of a fancy goldfish circling in a bowl which seemed to come out of nowhere. The chiffon of George's mother's dress floated around her knees a bit like goldfish tails, Lola reflected, although its color wasn't orange. She didn't think that was it. It didn't matter. She held her hand up to the car window but the family had already turned away.

They were in the habit of sleeping together, one night or two, on weekends, at his place or hers. She cleaned her apartment every Thursday evening. He rarely actually cleaned, but he was not a man who made messes. Sometimes Lola cleaned his bathroom when she was there, and he made no comment about this.

She found him very sexy. He had the kind of features that are described as chiseled. He was young and full of desire. When they made love he made mumbling noises she found exquisitely endearing.

His mumbling did not turn easily into words. He was not an articulate person, but she got around this. She found she could coax things out of him. She would say, on the telephone, during some brief separation, "do you miss me?" and he would reply, in an indulgent voice, with the inflection almost of a question, "yes . . ." And she would keep right on. "Do you love me?" she would risk, and he would say "mm-hmm" in the affirmative, which reminded her of the sweet noises he made when they had sex. He tolerated all of this without complaint, which she construed to mean he liked it, although as he enunciated his answers less and murmured them more she knew the game was winding down. Sooner or later they changed the subject.

He was not sentimental, but he was not unkind. He held her hand at the movies, squeezing tight during the scary parts.

When Lola tried to pick her mother's brain about George she responded in a guarded way, as if she did not trust what she might say. After the second divorce, during her bitter period, she had compared herself and her marriages to an equation: one plus two equals zero, she said. Lola remembered this now, talking to her, and thought immediately of George and his head for numbers.

Lola took her mother's reserve for cautious optimism, and gave her an extra long, extra tight embrace when they parted. Even as they hugged, an image flashed before Lola of two hands pulling hair back into a ponytail, the hair and the hands seemingly paler than her own, and this one she thought she must have dreamed and only just remembered. It made no sense. She lingered on it, trying to place it, played it and replayed it like a piece of film, until she and her mother separated and it went away again.

She asked her friends at work about George too, finding herself suddenly interested in how other people saw him, having reached the stage in love when she realized that she was not the only person in the world who had seen this person move and talk and smile. The girls at work had spoken to him on the phone, seen him come into the office. They'd watched him wait for his turn to talk to Lola when she was busy at the window. They reported that he always seemed so relaxed, never fidgety—they were used to dealing with so many fidgety people there—and he seemed cheerful and considerate, and was obviously crazy about Lola, the way he talked to her, looked at her, all the time he spent with her. So what was he *really* like, they said, and giggled. She tried to tell them but found she didn't have words that would add to what they already knew. The problem, she protested, was that she didn't know how serious he was, or how serious he wanted to be. Why don't you ask him, they said. I'm afraid to, she said, and they all nodded.

"Take it slow," said Cassandra, a woman who'd had a series of relationships that had all gone bad for no clear reason, and as she said this they all nodded again, gravely, each reminded of Cassandra's problem. "Take it slow, that's all I can say," she said, and then she blinked, and stared into space, as if she really couldn't think of anything else to say. How will I know? thought Lola. How slow is slow?

And so Lola practiced patience and affection, and things continued pleasantly with the two young lovers. Gradually, one variable did change, but by its nature it evaded immediate detection. Lola's distraction grew.

One Friday evening they sat down to have dinner together, and as they unfolded their menus the vision of a dusty book being taken down from a shelf absorbed Lola's attention so that it took her a long time to decide what she wanted, which bothered George because he was hungry. Then when the waitress tried to take their order, all Lola was able to think about was a pair of old sneakers with frayed shoelace ends, and she ended up telling George to go ahead and order first.

He asked her how her entree was, but she was busy at that moment with a postcard, specifically with the postmark on its corner, the wavy purple lines bleeding onto the stamp. She noticed too that one of her nostrils was partially blocked so that when the talk fell quiet her breathing made a sound like wind blowing sand in the desert. Moving on to discuss their weekend plans, she found the discussion interrupted by a stucco wall, coarse in appearance, with tendrils of vine crossing it. It took nearly a minute to get around that wall. Finally, George spoke.

"Hey, are you feeling all right?"

She looked right at him, eyes shining, wide awake.

"It's just that you've been acting kind of funny lately."

"I know," she said, "I know," trying to think how to explain it to him. "Maybe I should see a neurologist." She had, actually, thought about this just the other day. She worked, after all, in a doctor's office. It seemed natural enough to think of this.

"What?"

"A neurologist or maybe even a psychiatrist!" she said.

"God, Lola, no. I mean, you're not feeling that—that bad, are you?"

"No, it's not that I feel bad—"

"I mean, you do feel okay, don't you—you just seem—kind of distracted—is all."

"Yes, yes, I'm okay. That's exactly it, I'm distracted, it's the strangest thing."

"You're okay." He reached across the table and squeezed her hand, firmly and a long time, and looked into her eyes with great kindness, and Lola was going to explain more about the distraction business but then she didn't want to spoil the moment by saying anything. And she thought maybe she should just be happy that George didn't think her problem was really a problem. Maybe she should just feel glad, and leave it at that.

Then she noticed that her nostril now sounded a little like the long whiny cry of a baby. The sound was inside her head, though, not something George could hear.

From there they rode home together in his car, the silence between them like a long-married silence to her, though she thought perhaps not to him. Driving along without talking was fortunate for Lola because it provided cover for her meanderings. In an attentive moment she turned to look at him, and noting his business-like stare through the windshield she decided, for his sake, not to let herself daydream so much anymore, but then immediately saw the silliness in this, how it was a bit like that old king who stood on the shore telling the tide not to come in.

Tides—she saw waves unfolding on a smooth beach in perfect silence, small waves seen from far away, that crept and crept, forward and forward. What are the tides of life? she wondered. Where are those beaches?

She thought of palm tree beaches on travel brochures. Maybe this was what she and George needed, a vacation in some warm exotic love-spot, to bring their relationship to a head, a place without distractions where he would have to focus on her to the exclusion of all else, just a lot of sun and sand, and drinks with little umbrellas in garish colors—brightly, artificially colored like the countries on a map. They could be in one of those countries, in a bright pink or blue country where no one spoke English but them, and he still probably wouldn't say the things she was waiting to hear. She imagined herself lying on those faraway sands, some kind of ukulele music in the background, or maybe a steel drum band up on the veranda of the hotel, trying to sip at her drink except that the umbrella was getting in the way, and there was George, lying right next to her, as expected, only when he opened his mouth to speak all that came out was the local patois, and she couldn't understand a word. He had gone native.

But that was a dream. She was not on some island at all but here in George's car, floating along on the highway. She got a whiff of him suddenly, the smell of him that she was used to up close, her nose in his neck, that soapy, faintly salty and something else smell that she was sure wasn't quite like anyone else's, only now it was coming somehow right through his clothes. How could it do that, she wondered, or was she just imagining it? But how can you imagine a smell, a subtle smell? Imagine, she requested of herself, imagine life without the smell of him, imagine life without being able to imagine him. Think about life without the look or sound of him, without going to restaurants with him and having lunch down on the patio. Without the touch or skin of him. Nobody to make French toast for on Sunday mornings. I have to love him just the way he is! she protested, hearing herself addressing, of all people, her mother, who hovered before her now, smiling her strange, unyellowing, denture-wide smile. Mom! she pleaded. Does he love me? And then her mother's smile seemed to weaken, the taut edges of it pulling in. She didn't like being put on the spot. Of course he loves you, came her answer, but only because Lola dragged it out of her. It lacked sincerity, seemed to float by like an echo of harp music carried off on the breeze, and Lola, in fact, in the next instant, saw a picture of exactly that, a heavy, weeping harp trimmed in glinting Baroque, the strings beaded with dew drops of light, and all rippling with sorrow, and it was the first uninvited vision she'd had in a long time that made any sense to her at all.

Mother, she said, and behind the harp she saw clouds made out of cotton wool, and veils of tulle a bride might wear, drifting over everything. She looked down at her own feet in white shoes of lace and tiny pearls, and there she was, at last, never a bridesmaid, always a bride, and her mother was there of course as mothers must be, and Lola was climbing, climbing into her mother's lap, gathering her big white dress behind her. Climbing like a child up over her mother's knees, like a little girl again, or at least a bit younger, a teen, a blushing bride, the bloom of youth upon her apple cheek.

And crying suddenly, burying her face in her mother's goldfish-chiffon dress, crying about love but not about joy. It's George, she told her mother but her mother already knew. Why? she asked, why? Why doesn't anyone ever tell you that love, the love you wait for your whole life, that love can be old even when it's new? Even at its very beginning, dry, old as death.

The car squeaked to a stop, and George pulled up on the parking brake.

"We're here," he said.

"No we're not."

"What?"

Lola saw a glass overturned on a tablecloth, the damp spot spreading.

"Lola?"

She saw dust rising before a push-broom, and the rhythm of the broom, nudge, nudge, across the floor.

"Lola, what the hell is wrong with you?"

She stared down into the gut of a toilet. White, disappearing gut.

"Honey, hey"—softer now— "hey, are you all right?"

The frond of a fern brushed her cheek. She had the sensation of rising from dreams, head warm against the pillow, with the thought, you are almost awake, you are almost awake.

"Lola," he said, "please, talk to me."

She felt a hushed, empty feeling, like the streets of her old neighborhood in the evening after the children had gone inside.

Bit and Piece

What if her life was not a story? "Story" wasn't what she meant—she poured herself a second glass of wine, which doubled the quantity she drank each day for her health, and as she did so she leaned into the kitchen counter, felt its edge against her hipbone and remembered the strange fact of the skeleton inside her skin, and then forgot it again. Story wasn't it—plot was what she meant. Could she get away with a life without a plot?

Thinking about these sorts of words was not a pastime for her; she was a registered nurse who worked for a pair of dermatologists. She was a bright person who read the paper and followed a science writing blog and kept a journal when she went on vacation.

She rolled the wine in the glass and saw the clinging lines there that she knew were called cords but which seemed the wrong word for them, though she supposed tricky things like that would always get inadequate names. Was her story like that, a cop-out metaphor? Would her life be like cords on a wineglass, or the shoulder of a road, or could it have its own name like the hem of a skirt?

She thought she had reached the age when her life either needed to tell a story or it wouldn't, and her work for the dermatology practice, encouraging people with acne and skin cancer, wasn't it. Her life came to her not with any real narrative structure but rather in bits and pieces, a bit here and a piece there, arriving randomly, separated by days, weeks, or even years, decades.

She rolled the wine and looked at the cords and here's what she had: she had the way the dimples of a certain sewer cover had looked, a grid of diminutive puddles from recent rain and dotted with cherry blossom petals which she had at first mistaken for bits of broken glass. She had the image of a man laying his arm out the window of his pickup truck with his wrist draped over the side-view mirror. She had the hair just above her ankle that she'd missed when shaving her legs. She had the fisherman she'd dated, to whom she said: I don't think you're a keeper, I think you're catch-and-release. Besides she hadn't liked that funny thing about his eyebrows but wasn't about to tell him that. How many relationships had gone south in the world because of things like funny eyebrows you didn't want to spend the rest of your life looking at?

She had her mother's favorite song, "Stardust," and the way that it always made her think of cafés in Paris and all the things she'd never do including sitting in a café in Paris. Billie Holiday's rendition of "Autumn in New York," which she had heard only once but once was enough, had the same effect. It didn't matter if it was New York, or Paris, or even Rio de Janeiro when she heard "The Girl From Ipanema." And she always wondered if you had to go live those things, or if you could just imagine them, if it was enough to think of them even if you didn't know what they were really like.

She had the fact that her bedroom was mostly shades of blue. She had the tattoo she'd almost gotten once but didn't, and now she knew she never would. She had a memory of a stormy birthday, driving her car in and out of thundershowers in Florida or maybe Georgia, her cheeks sticky with tears and she couldn't remember why now, and that was the day she had seen not one but two rainbows, one ahead and one behind her, so she stopped the car on the side of the interstate to get out and look back and forth between them and the air was both oven-hot and misty, strange to breathe in. And there was the first time she'd heard a hummingbird—never saw it but heard the fierce blur of its wings around her as she hung a bright red dress on the line to dry, which the bird mistook for a huge flower. There was the way she'd worn a certain silver-and-marcasite ring for years, and then her friend Ginny gave her a nicer one but it made her feel strangely sad. There was the way she used to have to help her mother from the car, swiveling her into the wheelchair, the weight of her, which was different from how it had been doing the same thing with patients back when she worked in the hospital, because it was her own mother. In those suspended moments, her mother's breathing near her ear was too weak to feel on her skin but was audible, barely, like the panting of a bird.

 She was familiar with numerous generalizations—the many shades of green found in any lawn, the soothing effect of the sound of trickling water, the fact that people fail to notice clouds much from day to day. And other things which she thought might have the ring of general truth to them or might be, instead, particular to her, she couldn't tell: the way sometimes, walking, she'd notice the roll of the motion through her hips, which had to be different from what men felt when they walked, and perhaps was not something other women noticed either; or the way, sitting on a beach or a park bench with the sun on the back of her neck, she'd have a sudden image of the planets arrayed around the sun and herself there on the bright side of the earth, as if she had somehow been miniaturized and stepped into a tabletop model of the solar system.

Some of her questioning came down to this very problem, how much she shared and how much she could claim for her own in this whole matter of plot and story. Did other women, for example, walk past shop windows as if studying the wares on display when in fact, sometimes, they were just watching their own reflection? The only way to ever know would be to get on the other side of that glass, and get a close enough look at their eyes to see where they were focused.

But there were thoughts, and moments, that were hers alone: lying in bed, awake for some reason before it was light, hearing the first bird sing for dawn, long, long minutes before any others joined in, and knowing that although the same thing was happening all the time anywhere the sun was about to come up, this was the one singing-for-dawn bird where she was, the only one, the one that she, and perhaps no one else, was hearing. The room was deep gray around her, so she kept her eyes closed, hugged the pillow closer, and it was just her and that bird.

She continued to lie there, and she started thinking about her fisherman. There was more to the business with the fisherman than she was letting on, but it still didn't add up to a story, that was the point about the fisherman, that he did not add up. She had been a while without male companionship when she met him, and so it was nice to have someone to go to dinner with, and he was a pleasant man, and she could get turned on when they started kissing though it wasn't so much the fisherman himself who turned her on, but the strength of his desire, and that, she knew, would not provide a lasting basis for sexual relations. And when she looked into his eyes across a restaurant table, she felt she was not seeing much there except a great deal of presumption about her.

She lived both with men and without them, off and on, on and on. With and without had started to feel like the same thing. It was as if she couldn't remember, sometimes, if there were men or there were not men.

There were reminders—one day in the supermarket, she'd turned from a box of rice pilaf, wondering if the inclusion of a spice packet really justified charging three dollars for it, when she saw a beautiful blond boy of maybe seventeen coming down the aisle, and the hair on top of his head was bleached so white by the sun that it made her weak. She forgot all about rice. After a minute she went wandering off to find whatever it was she'd gone there for.

She missed holding the fisherman's hand in the movie theater, but went to matinees, stubbornly, by herself.

She wouldn't do any more blind dating (which was how she'd met the fisherman). Blind dating was aptly named, she thought, in that it blinded you, briefly, to who somebody was as you gazed at him over an overpriced cup of tea, earnestly trying to see him as something you brought into the coffee bar with you, and hoping you likewise matched the idea of you that he brought in with him.

Where was all this going? She didn't want it to deteriorate into some sour rag on men. Whatever her story was, if there was one, it wasn't about them. Especially at the moment, when loneliness was up but libido was down, and exercise, including her little weight-training routine, had taken the place of romance. It had been wonderful to watch her body change, the definition appearing at her arms and shoulders, so subtle and so slow. It was a private pleasure, not something she talked about. The ultimate, perhaps, in self-indulgence, and the word *narcissus* was on the tip of her tongue. But maybe that was the problem? If a life lacked plot, lacked real narrative, what did that leave you with but aimless, fruitless self-absorption?

Is that all I have? she wondered. Is that who I am? But weren't questions of identity supposed to be settled already, sometime in one's early twenties, according to the Erickson she'd been forced to commit to memory back in nursing school?

Hold up, she thought. She set her nearly empty wineglass on the counter. She told herself, back up a minute, back to where we were. She closed her eyes. She had: the undeniable beauty of Dutch flower paintings. A strange affection for humid weather. An admiration for archaeologists, gardeners, and pastry chefs. A mole on her cheek that she'd picked at as a child until it looked like a freckle. A line of poetry she'd written as a teenager that she still thought was good, and which still conjured the scene, viewed from the passenger seat of a slow-moving car: *falling snow unfocuses the trees across the park*. She'd shown the poem to her college English teacher and he said, 'Why do you want to go to nursing school?' But that was the last of that.

She'd give anything to have her mother alive again, so she could lift her from the car to the wheelchair.

She blinked her eyes open, saw the potholders hanging on the kitchen wall. She poured an inch of wine. She pressed her hip against the counter again but did not think, this time, of the bones inside her skin.

Her mind fell blank for a minute, although minds are never really blank. And then she thought how there was, not too long ago, a carpenter as well as a fisherman.

He did a little work on her house and on other houses up and down the street. He was a neighborhood guy, homegrown, it was as if he had sprung up like a beanstalk in the garden. He wasn't beautiful, he wasn't smart, but he was awfully, awfully nice. The straightforward type, fundamentally safe, the kind of guy who loves his mom and dad. She suddenly found she needed a new kitchen faucet, and discovered a problem with her screen door, and realized she wanted some new shelving in a couple of places.

He was big, six-foot-four, and his eyes looked tired from too many years working in the sun. His beard could have stood a little trimming in her opinion. He was the mistake she made when she tried to make love to a friend.

It was before she met the fisherman. She was more cocky then. She felt girlie all over telling him sex on the beach was not just the name of a drink, telling him, if you can't fuck your friends, who can you fuck? She got him to drive out to the island to go camping with her. Crossing the causeway, with the seagulls wheeling around them and the sun blinding on the blue water, the sky and sea seemed so huge, so full of possibility. She felt flush with female power saying to him, don't tell me more than you want me to know, and whatever you do, don't fall in love with me. He was the only man she'd ever said this to.

When they made love she closed her eyes, so she could imagine something more somehow. When they came home, she ate the wrong foods for a week and watched a lot of cable TV, paying attention even during the commercials.

Could it be that her story was no more than the story of the carpenter and the fisherman? And maybe it was not even that—if she closed her eyes and tried to think of *his face*, who would she see? She tried, and couldn't conjure any man's face.

No story, no story. She scratched her butt and sighed out loud and drained the wine and set it down. She stared at the stain of red visible in the dip at the bottom of the glass where it met the stem.

Time to back up again, back up. She backed up one last time and this is what she had: the view out the window of an airplane, ascending, lifted into a sky field of popcorn clouds. A fondness for the names of horses, just the names, like *sorrel roan*, and *chestnut mare*. One beautiful silk hand-painted dress, in muted rose and indigo, which draped like curtains of water from a fountain. A single image from some long ago family vacation—they'd visited Indian mounds, and she could still see the soft roundness of the grassy humps undulating into the distance.

There was the public television nature show about Antarctica that she'd seen, with the adorable penguins, but then the seals ate the penguins.

There was the hugeness of the full moon when it first rises.

There was the importance of being nice to people when you didn't feel like it.

There was the feeling of falling asleep, surrendering the layers.

There was the way, when her watch battery went dead, she felt a little lost on her way to the store to replace it.

There was, there was, there was.

She could keep thinking of things, always think of more things, but when would it be enough?

This time her mind really did go blank, as blank, in any case, as a mind can be, all blurred and thick, and this time she leaned into the counter but she didn't feel a thing, and she didn't hear the refrigerator compressor kick on and she didn't see the light change in the kitchen as a cloud passed off the sun, making the yellow walls more yellow and laying slats of gold across the floor.

She took her eyes from the empty glass on the counter, and looked at the ceiling but only because she had to look somewhere.

It would never add up. It was like fishermen and carpenters.

And so? What now? It was no good to keep thinking of different little things, they were all the same, they were interchangeable, coming up with another or another would not take her anywhere else. She would not do it anymore. She wouldn't feel sorry for herself because that would be ridiculous. She'd just have to live with it. This was where she was now, this was what she had learned. But she felt she had less than what she started with.

Her breathing felt heavy to her, a great effort, the breaths falling from her like leaden things. She remembered something her friend Ginny said once, philosophically, about a mutual acquaintance of theirs, *we all have to be some way*—it didn't help. She lifted her shoulders, to inhale. Her chest didn't want to stretch. She concentrated and made herself breathe in. And then she had: the way, driving in her car, if she saw honeysuckle blooming up ahead, she'd start to time her breathing to get the biggest possible whiff of it as she went by.

She saw the light on the kitchen floor and it was the color of honeysuckle. She caught on this, thinking of the word, honeysuckle.

She kept breathing. She decided to sit down at the kitchen table. She crossed her legs and rocked her ankle in the air, staring at the floor. She kept thinking. She thought: all right, for now—the smell of honeysuckle at the end of May.

For now. The breaths came easier, and she stopped being conscious of them. She watched the light on the floor, the color of it.

And this is what she had: she had honeysuckle, and she had beautiful blond boys and full moons and shades of green and Ginny's voice, and a silk dress and a sorrel roan, and her mother slipping into the wheelchair, out of her arms, and the sound of falling water, and one singing-for-dawn bird.

She had honeysuckle, lots of it, the sight and smell and taste of it, when as a child she'd stood before the great mass that spilled over the garden wall, and learned to lick the drop of nectar quivering from the pistil of each bloom.

Acknowledgments

I am so grateful to so many: the Maryland State Arts Council; the Kimmel Harding Nelson Center for the Arts; everyone who saw me through George Mason University's MFA program; the late Gloria Oden, who long ago took one look at my poems and pointed out that some writers are good at poetry but some are good at prose and had I ever tried writing a short story?; the patient readers who have nourished my work over the years, especially Linda Benson, Leslie Degnan, Robin Farabaugh, Deborah Linder, Nicole Pekarske, Henry Sloss, and my sisters Jane and Lucy; my dedicated, caring editor Kevin Watson; and most of all to Jim, who is like brackets around everything, the comma between my adjectives, the em dash of my heart. He is all kinds of punctuation.

Sally Shivnan's fiction and essays have appeared in *The Georgia Review, Antioch Review, Glimmer Train, Rosebud*, and other journals, and in anthologies including *The Best American Travel Writing* and Travelers' Tales *Best Travel Writing*. Her travel essays have been featured in *The Washington Post, Miami Herald, Nature Conservancy Magazine, Washingtonian, Saturday Evening Post, baltimore.org*, and many other publications and websites. She also broadcasts her bi-weekly "Prose and Poetry" radio program for blind listeners, available for streaming at the Radio Reading Network of Maryland. She was the winner of the 2011 Travel Classics International Travel Writers Contest and a Maryland State Arts Council grant, among other awards. She teaches creative writing at University of Maryland Baltimore County (UMBC), is currently at work on a novel, and can be found at SallyShivnan.com.